"*The Seduction of Lord Stone* is romantic, emotional, sexy and funny. In fact, everything I have come to expect from Anna Campbell. I'm looking forward to reading the other Dashing Widows' stories." —*RakesandRascals.com*

"With her marvelous combination of humor and poignancy Anna Campbell writes in such a way that every story of hers has a special meaning and remains like a sentimental keepsake with those fortunate enough to read her work!" —*JeneratedReviews.com*

"*Lord Garson's Bride* is a well written and passionate story that touched my heart and sent my emotions on a rollercoaster ride. I particularly recommend this book for fans of convenient marriages, and those who enjoy seeing a deserving character find out that love is lovelier the second time around." —*Roses Are Blue Reviews*

"Campbell immediately hooks readers, then deftly reels them in with a spellbinding love story fueled by an addictive mixture of sharp wit, lush sensuality, and a wealth of well-delineated characters."—*Booklist, starred review, on A Scoundrel by Moonlight*

"With its superbly nuanced characters, impeccably crafted historical setting, and graceful writing shot through with scintillating wit, Campbell's latest lusciously sensual, flawlessly written historical Regency ... will have romance readers sighing happily with satisfaction."—*Booklist, Starred Review, on What a Duke Dares*

"Campbell makes the Regency period pop in the appealing third Sons of Sin novel. Romantic fireworks, the constraints of custom, and witty banter are combined in this sweet and successful story."—*Publishers Weekly on What a Duke Dares*

"Campbell is exceptionally talented, especially with plots that challenge the reader, and emotions and characters that are complex and memorable."—*Sarah Wendell, Smart Bitches Trashy Books, on A Rake's Midnight Kiss*

"A lovely, lovely book that will touch your heart and remind you why you read romance."—*Liz Carlyle, New York Times bestselling author on What a Duke Dares*

"Campbell holds readers captive with her highly intense, emotional, sizzling and dark romances. She instinctually knows how to play on her readers' fantasies to create a romantic, deep-sigh tale."—*RT Book Reviews, Top Pick, on Captive of Sin*

"Don't miss this novel - it speaks to the wild drama of the heart, creating a love story that really does transcend class."—*Eloisa James, New York Times bestselling author, on Tempt the Devil*

"*Seven Nights in A Rogue's Bed* is a lush, sensuous treat. I was enthralled from the first page to the last and still wanted more."—*Laura Lee Guhrke, New York Times bestselling author*

"No one does lovely, dark romance or lovely, dark heroes like Anna Campbell. I love her books."—*Sarah MacLean, New York Times bestselling author*

"It isn't just the sensuality she weaves into her story that makes Campbell a fan favorite, it's also her strong, three-dimensional characters, sharp dialogue and deft plotting. Campbell intuitively knows how to balance the key elements of the genre and give readers an irresistible, memorable read."—*RT Book Reviews, Top Pick, on Midnight's Wild Passion*

"Anna Campbell is an amazing, daring new voice in romance."—*Lorraine Heath, New York Times bestselling author*

"Ms. Campbell's gorgeous writing a true thing of beauty..."—*Joyfully Reviewed*

"She's the mistress of dark, sexy and brooding and takes us into the dens of iniquity with humor and class."—*Bookseller-Publisher Australia*

"Anna Campbell is a master at drawing a reader in from the very first page and keeping them captivated the whole book through. Ms. Campbell's books are all on my keeper shelf and *Midnight's Wild Passion* will join them proudly. *Midnight's Wild Passion* is a smoothly sensual delight that was a joy to read and I cannot wait to revisit Antonia and Nicholas's romance again."—*Joyfully Reviewed*

"Ms. Campbell gives us...the steamy sex scenes, a heroine whose backbone is pure steel and a stupendous tale of lust and love and you too cannot help but fall in love with this tantalizing novel."—*Coffee Time Romance*

"Anna Campbell offers us again, a lush, intimate, seductive read. I am in awe of the way she keeps the focus tight on the hero and heroine, almost achingly so. Nothing else really exists in this world, but the two main characters. Intimate, sensual story with a hero that will take your breath away."—*Historical Romance Books & More*

ALSO BY ANNA CAMPBELL

Claiming the Courtesan

Untouched

Tempt the Devil

Captive of Sin

My Reckless Surrender

Midnight's Wild Passion

The Sons of Sin series:

Seven Nights in a Rogue's Bed

Days of Rakes and Roses

A Rake's Midnight Kiss

What a Duke Dares

A Scoundrel by Moonlight

Three Proposals and a Scandal

The Dashing Widows:

The Seduction of Lord Stone

Tempting Mr. Townsend

Winning Lord West

Pursuing Lord Pascal

Charming Sir Charles

Catching Captain Nash

Lord Garson's Bride

The Lairds Most Likely:

The Laird's Willful Lass

The Laird's Christmas Kiss

The Highlander's Lost Lady

Christmas Stories:

The Winter Wife

Her Christmas Earl

A Pirate for Christmas

Mistletoe and the Major

A Match Made in Mistletoe

The Christmas Stranger

Other Books:

These Haunted Hearts

Stranded with the Scottish Earl

PURSUING LORD PASCAL

THE DASHING WIDOWS BOOK 4

ANNA CAMPBELL

Serenade Publishing

ISBN: 978-0-6483987-6-9

Cover design: By Hang Le

Print editions published by Serenade Publishing
www.serenadepublishing.com

To my dear friend Deborah Allen.

PROLOGUE

Woodley Park, Leicestershire, November 1828

To a farmer, even winter's dreary beginning had its purpose.

Or so Amy, Lady Mowbray, told herself as she stared out of the morning room window onto the landscape of her childhood. It was early on a gray day. Around her, the old house was blessedly quiet. That would change, once everyone was up.

Nash friends and family gathered to celebrate the christening of her brother Silas's fourth child. The revels had extended late last night, but Amy, used to rising with the birds to tramp her fields at Warrington Court, couldn't sleep.

So she didn't expect the door to open and reveal

Sally Cowan, Countess of Norwood. "Lady Mowbray, I didn't think anyone else was awake."

Amy didn't know Sally well. Recently the attractive widow had become friends with her sister-in-law Morwenna. Morwenna mostly lived in seclusion in Portsmouth, but she and Sally both supported a charity for indigent naval widows.

"I don't keep sophisticated hours, Lady Norwood." Anything but. Lately the sheer predictability of her days had begun to pall.

When she was a girl, she'd become interested in scientific agriculture, and since then, the rhythms of planting and harvest had ruled her life. Her brief marriage seven years ago had caused barely a hiccup in the endless seasonal work.

"I don't either." Lady Norwood closed the door and ventured into the room. "I'm looking for something to read. I know Caro keeps the latest novels in here. I won't disturb you."

Amy rarely sought female company, although she loved her sister Helena who slept upstairs, no doubt blissfully, in her husband's arms. But something about the bleak, lonely dawn left her dissatisfied with solitude. "No need to go. Would you like a cup of tea?"

Lady Norwood cast her a searching look, before a smile of startling charm lit her face. She wasn't exactly pretty. Her long, thin nose had a definite kink, and her eyes and mouth were too large for her face, but she was dauntingly stylish. Next to her, Amy always felt a complete frump.

This morning was a case in point. Lady Norwood wore a filmy cream gown, trimmed with bands of satin ribbon, deep green to match her remarkable eyes. With her loosely gathered fair hair, she looked like the spirit of spring, even as the year moved into winter.

Whereas Amy had dredged a frock ten years out of date from the cupboard in the bedroom she always used at Woodley Park. She'd assumed at this hour, she wouldn't run into any other guests. She was sharply conscious that the dress was faded and worn, and too loose for her. At twenty-five, she was slimmer than she'd been at sixteen.

"Thank you. I'd love a cup of tea. Morwenna speaks so fondly of you, Lady Mowbray. I was looking forward to this house party as a chance to get to know you."

Amy crossed the room to the tray a footman had just brought in and poured two cups. "Please call me Amy. Lady Mowbray is my late husband's mother." Who lived in Brighton, and fussed over her ten pugs, and found little common ground with the practical young woman her son had married.

Lady Norwood turned something as mundane as accepting a cup and saucer into an act of breathtaking grace. Amy stifled an unworthy pang of envy. Not even her best friend—if she had one—would credit her with a shred of elegance. Somehow this morning, that seemed a shame.

"Very well, Amy. And you must call me Sally." She sipped her tea as the door swung open.

"Morwenna," Amy said in surprise, placing her tea on a side table and stepping forward to embrace her lovely, fragile sister-in-law. The body in her arms was so thin, Amy feared it might break if she wasn't careful. "You're up early."

"You know I don't sleep much these days." The willowy brunette focused her large blue eyes on Sally and managed a smile. "Good morning, Sally."

"Good morning, Morwenna."

"Have some tea." Amy filled another delicate Wedgwood cup. There were four on the tray. The footman must have guessed she'd have company. "I'm sorry you had a bad night. If it's so difficult for you to see the family, you don't have to come to these gatherings. Everyone would understand—although we'd miss you."

Bitterness twisted Morwenna's lips as she took her tea and sat on a brocade chaise longue near the fire. Although all three women were widows, only Morwenna wore mourning. The dense black emphasized her ghostly pallor. "I doubt it. I'm well aware that I'm a constant reminder of sorrow."

Grief stabbed Amy. Sharp. Painful. Accepted, but unsoftened by time. "The sorrow is always there for us, whether you're here or not."

Robert Nash, Morwenna's husband and Amy's

brother, had been lost at sea four years ago in a skirmish with pirates off the Brazilian coast. At first, because Robert had been such a larger-than-life character, everyone who loved him had held out hope of his survival. But as month followed month, the grim truth of his death became undeniable reality. When the navy had ordered him into the South Atlantic, Robert was newly married to this charming Cornish girl, who had since become a beloved member of the Nash family.

Morwenna cast her a sad smile—sad smiles were her stock in trade these days. "I apologize. I didn't mean to imply his family had forgotten him. I know you haven't—but you all have other concerns, other people to occupy you."

Amy hid a wince. Because she didn't. Not really. Her estate ran like clockwork, and her steward and staff were so well trained in her methods that they could manage without her, indefinitely if necessary.

Devil take this strange humor. Why on earth was she so discontented? Envying Sally's style. Even envying Morwenna, who at least had known love before losing it.

Amy and her late husband had been good friends, despite the age difference, but the stark truth was that she'd married him to join him in his farming experiments. When Sir Wilfred Mowbray passed away five years ago, agriculture lost a great innovator. Amy had grieved over a man more mentor than husband.

Her marriage had been her choice, but on this

dismal day, she couldn't help thinking life should hold more than cattle breeding and crop rotation. And she'd never thought that before.

"Kerenza enjoys seeing her cousins." Sally sat next to Morwenna. "I know you miss Robert, but you're lucky to have a daughter to love."

"Yes, she's a darling. I wish Robert had known he had a child. She's so like him."

"And becoming more so," Amy said. The whole family found a measure of consolation in Robert's bright, pretty daughter.

"I would dearly have loved children," Sally said in a muffled voice, her mobile features uncharacteristically somber. She placed her teacup on the tray, and Amy was distressed to see that her hand trembled. "But God didn't see fit to bless me."

"I'm sorry," Morwenna said gently.

Sally shook her head. "Ten years of marriage, and no sign of a baby. Lord Norwood bore his disappointment bravely."

But nevertheless made that disappointment felt, Amy guessed.

"You could marry again, Sally," Morwenna said.

Amy saw Sally hide a shudder, confirming her vague impression that the Norwood marriage had been unhappy. She was curious, but even she, renowned for her tactlessness, couldn't ask a woman she hardly knew for intimate details. More was the pity. She had an inkling she and Sally might end up friends.

"No, thank you. I'm too old to take a man's orders, or change my ways to fit another person."

Morwenna struggled for a real smile. Amy almost wished she wouldn't. The effort involved made even someone watching feel tired. "But if you want children…"

Sally's shrug didn't mask her regret. "I have nieces and nephews. In fact, I'm going to bring my niece Meg out in London next season. I intend to dive into the social whirl and enjoy myself as much as a woman of my advanced years may."

To Amy's surprise, Morwenna gave a derisive snort that sounded like the vital girl Robert had married, rather than the wraith of recent years. "Only if your arthritis permits, you poor decrepit thing."

Reluctant humor tugged at Sally's lips. "Well, I'm no longer a giddy girl. Not that I had much chance to kick up my heels. My parents married me off at seventeen."

"And now you're only thirty," Morwenna said, showing more spirit than Amy had seen in ages. "Why not have some fun?"

"You're a great one to talk," Amy said, before she remembered that Morwenna needed delicate handling.

Morwenna paled, and her animation faded. "It's different for me."

"No, it's not," Amy said, justifying her reputation for blundering in where angels feared to tread, but unable to stay quiet. "I loved my brother, but you've mourned him for four years. He wouldn't want you moping around for the rest of your life. Why don't you go to London with Sally?"

As Morwenna frowned over what she clearly considered an outlandish suggestion, Sally clapped her hands together with enthusiasm. "Why don't you? I'd love a friend to go about with. Meg is a capable, sensible girl and won't need me hovering."

Morwenna glared at Amy. "And what about you?"

"Me?"

"Yes, you. You spend so much time stomping through your muddy fields that turnips are practically growing out of your hair—which, by the way, could do with some attention. As could your wardrobe."

Amy backed away until her hips bumped into the windowsill. "We're not talking about me."

"Yes, we are." Morwenna turned to Sally. "Amy could be really pretty if she made an effort and wore something apart from rags a beggar woman would disdain to put on her back."

"That's unfair," Amy protested, even as she reluctantly admitted that her dress today might deserve the criticism.

"Is it?" Morwenna's glance was scornful. "Did you find today's monstrosity in the back of a cupboard? Or did you steal it from the housemaids before they could use it as a duster?"

Amy flushed and shot Morwenna an annoyed look. "I think I prefer you cowed and miserable."

"You could come to London, too, Amy," Sally said

calmly. "I'd love to introduce you to my modiste and show you off at some parties. Morwenna's right. You're a pretty girl."

Amy was already shaking her head. "I won't fit into society."

"How do you know?" Morwenna said.

"I had a season, and I didn't take." Amy decided to go on the attack. "Anyway, why should I break out of my comfortable little rut when you won't?"

Morwenna's chin set in unexpected stubbornness. "I didn't say I wouldn't."

Sally looked startled, then pleased. "So you'll come?"

"Only if Amy does."

Sally's expression turned thoughtful. "I was talking to Fenella and Helena last night. They told me that once they came out of mourning for their first husbands, they formed a club called the Dashing Widows and set out to turn London on its ear."

Amy had long been familiar with the story. Eight years ago, her sister Helena, her sister-in-law Caroline, and their dear friend Fenella had cast aside old sorrows and danced and flirted their way into happy marriages. "It wasn't a club. It was more a…a pact."

"Can't we make such a pact?" Sally spread her hands. "I'm sure we three can be Dashing Widows, too, if we put our minds to it."

"I'm not particularly dashing, and I've got nothing to wear," Amy said, amazed at her spurt of disappointment. Perhaps her mood this morning hinted at a malaise deeper than temporary restlessness.

Sally stood in front of her and subjected her to a thorough and dispassionate examination. "You know, with the right clothes, and a bit more confidence, you could really shine."

A painful blush heated Amy's cheeks, and she shifted from one foot to the other. With her mop of tawny hair and dominating Nash nose, not to mention the fact that she'd always been far more interested in cattle than flirting, she'd never felt comfortable in society. She looked like her brother Silas, but unfortunately the quirky features that made him a draw for the ladies only turned her into an oddity. "I made a complete shambles of my season."

Morwenna came to stand beside Sally and conducted her own inspection, just as comprehensive. "That was years ago, and you didn't have Sally to help you."

"And you," Sally said.

Morwenna smiled. "And me."

Morwenna looked more alive than she had since receiving the news of Robert's death. Amy dearly loved her sister-in-law and couldn't bear to think of her languishing in a dark pit of grief all her life. Amy had never been in love—although when she was fourteen, she'd harbored a violent fit of puppy love for Lord Pascal, widely considered London's handsomest man.

Which made her adolescent interest a complete joke, given the graceless ragamuffin she'd been.

But she knew about love. It surrounded her—Silas and Caro, Helena and Vernon, her parents who had died together ten years ago in a carriage accident outside Naples. She didn't discount love's power to create joy.

Morwenna had suffered enough. Now she deserved new happiness. If that meant that Amy had to hang up her farm boots and put on her dancing slippers, she'd do it.

"You'll have your work cut out for you," she said drily.

Sally frowned. "No more of that talk. By the time I've finished with you, you're going to dazzle the ton. We'll tame that wild mane of hair and dress you in something bright that shows off your splendid figure. By heaven, you'll be the toast of Mayfair."

How extraordinary. Within minutes, she and Sally had gone from acquaintances to co-conspirators. At Warrington Court, Amy inhabited a largely masculine world. She wasn't used to cozy chats with other women. Especially cozy chats about fripperies like clothes and hair.

"So we're doing this?" She looked past Sally to Morwenna.

Amy was afraid of facing those critical crowds again, but also strangely excited. This felt like a new challenge, and she realized she badly needed one.

Morwenna straightened and met her eyes. Amy was used to seeing endless grief there. Now she caught a glimpse of something that looked like hope. If so, she didn't care if the fashionable multitudes shunned her.

Anything was worth it, if Morwenna came back to life.

"Yes," Morwenna said unhesitatingly.

Sally caught Amy and Morwenna's hands and laughed. "Then I hereby declare the return of the Dashing Widows. Watch out, London. We're on our way."

CHAPTER ONE

Raynor House, Mayfair, March 1829

*S*ometimes it was no fun to be London's handsomest man.

Gervaise Dacre, Earl Pascal, glanced across at the pretty blonde chit beside him in the line and struggled to hide his impatience for the dance to finish.

"It's quite a crush tonight," he said. He'd already flung usually reliable topics like the weather and last night's ball into the conversational impasse. They now lay bleeding and silent on the floor.

There was a long pause—not the first one—while the girl's blush turned an alarming shade of red. Then without meeting his eyes, she managed to say, "Yes," so softly that he had to lean closer to hear.

Miss Veivers was an heiress and accounted one of the diamonds of the season, but clearly the honor of sharing a contredanse with that magnificent personage Lord Pascal had rendered her incoherent. She was his third partner tonight, and he hadn't succeeded in coaxing more than a monosyllable out of any of them.

For a man in search of a wife, it was a depressing state of affairs. Last January's storm had left his estate in ruins. He needed cash, and he needed it quickly. He'd come up to Town, vowing he'd do anything to restore his fortune.

But surely there must be better alternatives than Miss Veivers and her pretty little airheaded friends.

Did London this season contain no women of sense? Clearly none had attended this extravagant ball to launch Lord and Lady Raynor's youngest daughter. When he'd waltzed with the overexcited Raynor girl, she'd nearly giggled him to death.

Bored, he glanced over the top of his partner's ridiculous coiffure. Why did females torture their hair into such God awful monstrosities? Half of Kew Gardens sprouted from the girl's elaborate brown curls. Across the room, he noticed a party of late arrivals.

Four pretty women in the first stare of fashion. He immediately recognized the tall blonde as Sally Cowan, who bore enough resemblance to the young miss in white to suggest a relationship. Probably aunt and niece. Beside them was a graceful brunette in buttercup yellow.

Last to step into the ballroom was a tall woman with tawny hair arranged with an elegant simplicity that set off her striking features. Her rich purple gown clung to her Junoesque figure with breathtaking precision. She reminded him of someone, although Pascal would swear they'd never met.

His heart crashed against his ribs, and he only just stopped himself stumbling. He who was lauded as a perfect dancer.

In a room full of fluttering, cooing doves, this woman had the presence and power of a swan floating across a moonlit lake.

How could he concentrate on half-baked girls when that luscious banquet of a female wandered into sight? Damn it, he had to find out who she was.

"L-Lord Pascal?" the chit in his arms stammered, the chit whose name he'd already forgotten. "Are you going to the Bartletts' ball tomorrow night? Mamma is most eager that we at…attend."

"I'm sure I'll be there." He was hardly aware what he said, as he took her hand to lead her up the line. He couldn't take his eyes off the superb creature standing beside Sally. Who the devil was she? He wasn't looking for a mistress, and the state of his finances meant he couldn't veer from his purpose. But by God, even across the crowded room, he wanted her.

"Oh," the chit said breathlessly. "Oh, doubtless we'll see you there."

"Doubtless." He wondered idly what he'd agreed to. But he didn't wonder much. Most of his mind remained fixed on the tall woman, who had joined Lord and Lady Kenwick near the French doors, closed against the chilly night.

Brutal necessity insisted he pay court to one of the wellborn virgins brought to London to shine on the marriage mart. Every masculine impulse insisted he engage the attention of the woman in imperial purple.

The battle was brief, its outcome sure, even before it began.

He returned Miss Veivers—at last he remembered her name—to her parents and set off in pursuit of much more interesting prey.

"Stop picking at your gown," Sally hissed out of the corner of her mouth as they stood in a laughing group with Anthony and Fenella Townsend, and Fenella's handsome son Brandon Deerham.

Guiltily Amy forced her trembling hand down from where she'd been hauling at the low bodice. "It's too tight. And I feel half naked."

"For pity's sake, you look wonderful—and the dress is quite modest by London standards."

"Not by Leicestershire standards. And it's so bright."

"It is," Sally said. "And don't start fiddling with your hair instead. You said you liked it when my maid put it up like that."

"I do." She liked the dress, too, although she felt painfully self-conscious in the flashy color. "But it doesn't look like everyone else's hair."

Around her, she saw women whose hair was arranged into elaborate ringlets and knots. Hers was almost austere in its simplicity.

"No, and all the better for it. You've got a classical beauty. Make the most of it."

"I don't think I've got any beauty at all," she muttered under her breath, hoping Sally wouldn't hear. Over the last bustling week of modistes and milliners and maids poking and prodding at her, she'd learned that Sally had no tolerance for self-doubt. Given self-doubt was Amy's default position, she was surprised that their friendship survived. Even prospered.

"Of course you do," Morwenna said, proving she'd been eavesdropping. Last November's woebegone widow was impossible to recognize in the slender woman in spangled yellow sarsenet, who faced this glittering crowd with unexpected assurance. "You mightn't see it, but everyone else does, even when you're wearing faded chintz and farm boots, and you have mud on your face. You just need to believe you're beautiful."

"Thank you," Amy said, still unconvinced. Morwenna didn't understand what it was like to grow up as the only plain member of a good-looking family. Silas and Robert were both handsome men, and Helena, while unconventional in looks, was nonetheless striking. Whereas Amy had always felt like a cabbage set in the middle of a bouquet of roses. "I'll say one good thing for cattle and sheep—they don't care what you look like."

"You can't spend your life in a barn, Amy," Morwenna said. This week, she'd been as bossy as Sally. Amy didn't mind. It was wonderful to see her venturing back into life again, even if it meant sisterly nagging.

"Yes, I can."

"Nonsense," Fenella said, proving she'd been listening while her fine blue eyes scanned the ballroom. "You're a lovely girl, Amy, and it's about time you crept out from under your rock and showed the world your mettle."

Amy went back to plucking at her bodice, until a scowl from Sally made her drop her hand. "But people —men—keep staring. I feel like a fright."

"They're staring because you're a new face—and you look good enough to eat in that dress," Anthony Townsend, Lord Kenwick, said, proving he, too, lent an ear to Amy's cowardly havering. "In fact, may I have this dance, Amy? Otherwise, I doubt I'll have another chance all night."

"Really?"

"Trust us," Sally said with a sigh. "As if we'd let you make a fool of yourself."

"No, I can do that all by myself."

"Amy," Morwenna said sternly. "Hold your head up and dance with Anthony. And when gentlemen line up to dance with you, act as if you expected nothing else."

"Since when have you been such an expert on the ton?"

Morwenna had met Robert in Cornwall, and they'd married after a whirlwind courtship. He'd left for the South Atlantic before he had a chance to introduce his wife to London society. "I'll have you know that I was the belle of the Truro assemblies. This is just a larger, better dressed version. I can already see you're going to make a sensation. Enjoy it."

"I wish I was back talking about drainage with my steward," she mumbled.

As Sally rolled her eyes, Anthony took her hand. "Courage, lass."

She lifted her gaze to his and managed a smile. He towered over her. He towered over most people, and he'd never lost the bluff manners of his humble Yorkshire upbringing. But while he might look like a mountain, she'd long ago learned that he had a kind heart and a mind sharp enough to see past her grumbles to the sheer terror possessing her soul.

"Please promise you'll dance with me again if nobody else does."

The twitch of his mouth bolstered her failing

courage. "I promise. And so will Brandon. Won't you, my lad?"

Brandon, fair and beautiful like his mother, subjected Amy to a glance of unmistakable admiration. "Rather! Amy, you're looking tiptop. All the fellows will be knocked for six."

It was Fenella's turn to roll her eyes. "Brandon, I despair of your expensive Cambridge education. You used to speak the King's English."

Anthony sent his wife a fond glance. "It's nowt to worry about. He's just bang up to date, my love." He turned his attention back to Amy. "And I have to agree with him. You're as bonny as they come. Now let me show you off."

Amy let him lead her onto the floor. Fenella's family really were so kind. She sucked in a breath to calm the nervous gallop of her heart. What did it matter what London thought when she had such loving friends?

As she lined up opposite Anthony, she noticed Brandon and Meg taking the floor together. Seconds later, Fenella, Morwenna and Sally found partners.

She'd spent her life afraid of the ton's disparaging eye. But when she started to execute the steps—she'd spent the last month practicing dances she hadn't attempted since adolescence—giddy excitement gripped her. Not strong enough to banish uncertainty, but heady nonetheless.

Here she was at the center of London society. She had beautiful new clothes and friends set on her enjoyment. Who knew what adventures the next few weeks might bring? At the very least, she'd have something to remember when she went back to counting heifers and weighing oats on her estate.

By the time she'd danced a minuet with Anthony and a quadrille with Brandon, Amy was almost comfortable in her new clothes. It still amazed her quite how much attention and effort went into preparing a woman to appear at a ball that merely lasted a few hours. If she took this much time to dress at Warrington Court, the estate would fall into ruin.

Gradually her choking fear receded. The people she spoke to were nice to her, and nobody pointed a finger in her direction and shrieked "imposter!" Which didn't make her any less of an imposter in this glamorous milieu.

She even started to enjoy herself. The music was pretty; the dancing was fun once she stopped worrying about forgetting the steps; even a fashion ignoramus like her appreciated the beautiful clothing on display.

Best of all, Morwenna looked young and happy for the first time in four years. And the men in the room showed the excellent taste to clamor to dance with her.

Nor did Sally lack for partners. She always spoke as if she was at her last prayers, but the gentlemen seemed as eager to dance with her as with her pretty niece Meg.

So when Mr. Harslett, a man with an interesting take on using turnips as pig feed, deposited Amy back with Fenella and Anthony after their dance, she could almost pretend to poise. So silly to be scared of something as trivial as a ball. At this rate, she might even survive her London season without carrying too many scars away.

Then all that frail confidence fizzled to nothing. Striding toward her was the man she'd spent a couple of wretched years dreaming about when she was a silly girl. He'd fueled her romantic fantasies, until she hit sixteen and decided that life was real and practical, and adolescent foolishness served no purpose.

Anthony greeted Pascal with unalloyed pleasure. "Grand to see you."

"And you, Kenwick." Lord Pascal bowed briefly to Fenella. "Lady Kenwick."

"My lord," Fenella said with a pretty curtsy.

"Will you please introduce me to your lovely companion?"

Lovely companion? Amy almost looked around to see who he meant, even as those blue eyes leveled on her with unmistakable intent.

"Amy, may I present Lord Pascal?" Fenella said, shooting him a speculative glance. "Pascal, this is Amy, Lady Mowbray, down from Leicestershire for the season."

Automatically Amy extended her hand. When he took it in his and bowed, a strange current zapped through her as if she touched lightning. Bewildered, she told herself this was impossible, especially as they both wore gloves. But rational thought was elusive when such remarkable male beauty filled her view.

The hundreds of candles in the ballroom turned Lord Pascal to gold. Golden hair. Golden skin. Tall, perfectly proportioned body. Broad, straight shoulders. Narrow hips. Long legs. Cheekbones high and prominent. Lips so crisply cut that they could be sculpted from marble, if they weren't so sensual.

Such spectacular masculinity would make Michelangelo weep.

"Delighted, Lady Mowbray." His soft murmur set every nerve jangling with female awareness.

"Good evening, my lord," she said, shocked that the words emerged at all, let alone as steadily as they did.

With a spurt of relief, she realized that she wasn't sixteen anymore. By God, she could handle society. She could handle anything life threw at her. Here was proof. While butterflies and grasshoppers performed a mad ballet in her stomach, she faced down the man who had once turned her tongue-tied.

Her smile broadened as she stared into Lord Pascal's brilliant blue eyes. Dear heaven, that color was extraordinary, like a noon sky on a perfect summer day.

Those eyes warmed and turned predatory, and she

realized her hand still rested in his. Ten years ago—
good Lord, last week—she'd have jerked away, flustered and awkward. Not tonight. Tonight she remained
where she was and let herself drown in those azure
eyes.

"May I presume upon our new acquaintance and
ask for this waltz?"

"I'm engaged with Sir Brandon." With a flirtatious-
ness she'd never before attempted, she let her lashes
flutter down. She didn't mention that she and Pascal
had met before, if years ago. Why revive memories of
her clumsy younger self and spoil this chance to make
an old dream come true?

Pascal didn't even glance at Fenella's son. "I'm sure
he'll yield to my greater need."

"Greater need?" Amy slowly withdrew her hand.

"Sometimes a waltz can be a matter of life or death,
my lady."

Brandon turned away from Meg and smiled at Amy.
"Shall we?"

He must have missed the quiet exchange between
Amy and Pascal. She shivered with delight. His lordship's nonsense seemed even more delicious when
spoken privately in a public place.

"I'm claiming seniority," Pascal said with a smile.

"That's a dashed cheek," Brandon said good-
naturedly. "What's a fellow to do instead?"

"He can dance with his dear sweet mother," Fenella

said, taking his arm and casting a laughing glance at Amy and Lord Pascal.

"Always happy to dance with you, Mamma," Brandon said gallantly. "You're still the prettiest woman in the room."

"Are you sure, Brandon?" Amy asked, feeling bad for deserting him.

"That my mamma is a peach? I am indeed." He didn't sound like he minded too much missing out on partnering Amy.

"You're a good lad," Anthony said, clapping his son on the shoulder.

"You have my thanks, Sir Brandon." Pascal drew Amy toward the dance floor.

"Do I get any say in this?" she asked, with a breathless catch in her voice.

His arm slid around her waist, and he caught her hand in his, setting off another of those odd frissons. "Do you want to say no?"

He stared down at her as if he saw nobody else in this crowded ballroom. She had to work hard to summon a response. It really was the most extraordinary sensation, being this close to such physical splendor. Her girlhood self had been transfixed, but mostly at a distance. Now it turned out that grown-up Amy was even more susceptible to golden good looks and deep blue eyes. The music started, and for the first time, her steps fell into the rhythm without her conscious effort to count.

"Lady Mowbray, do you want to say no?"

She reminded herself that she was no longer a naïve, impressionable ninnyhammer. She'd been married. She ran a great estate. Her appearance was modish in the extreme. She owed it to Sally to demonstrate a modicum of polish.

Instinct told her to play at reluctance. It was a game she'd seen enacted often, although she'd never before felt equipped to join in. But the answer that emerged was short and honest. "No."

That striking face so far above hers—his perfect proportions hid quite how tall he was until you were right next to him—relaxed into a smile of masculine satisfaction. "That's what I hoped."

He swept her into a turn that left her dizzy. Yet feet that usually threatened to stumble kept her upright and moving.

Heat radiated everywhere they touched, and her heart raced with exertion and excitement. She could hardly believe it. Her first ball this season, and she danced with a man as close to a prince as any she was ever likely to meet.

Cinderella would be green with envy.

CHAPTER TWO

*P*ascal started his campaign the next afternoon. Last night's two dances had only whetted his curiosity about the new arrival to London. In between, he'd managed to find out what little society knew about the beguiling Lady Mowbray.

The lady was a widow, and now he understood that nagging feeling of familiarity. She was Silas Nash, Lord Stone's youngest sister. The Nashes were a famously clever family.

And Pascal's luck held beyond her brains and lack of an encumbering spouse. It seemed there was money. Unusually, most of the late Sir Wilfred Mowbray's property hadn't been entailed on his next male heir, but left to his young widow. With a generous portion from her Nash relatives, this lovely woman was nicely plump in the pocket.

Perhaps Pascal needn't marry a dimwitted heiress to restore the Dacre fortunes after all.

He'd also learned that she was staying with Sally in Half Moon Street. Which explained why he was currently standing on the elegant front steps of Norwood House.

The butler showed him to the drawing room and left to ascertain if Lady Mowbray was at home. The room was crammed with bouquets, and if only a fraction were for Lady Mowbray, it was clear that Pascal had competition. Even as he waited, footmen carried in at least another half dozen.

Etiquette limited a partner who was neither husband nor betrothed to two dances at a party. So last night, Pascal had watched as she'd danced every set, apart from his two, with one or another of London's fashionable numskulls. Most of whom he counted as his friends.

Now he scowled at the riot of color surrounding him. He restrained the urge to gather up every last flower, whomever they were meant for, and toss the lot into the street.

He possessed enough self-awareness to be surprised at his jealousy.

Lady Mowbray entered with the resolute strut he'd noticed last night. Most girls were taught to prance and mince, but Lady Mowbray, who wasn't much past girl-hood, despite being a widow, stalked into a room as if she knew where she was going, and meant to get there sooner rather than later. After ten years of society poppets, he liked how she moved.

"Lord Pascal, how lovely of you to call." The thick mane of leonine hair was caught up in a loose knot that made his fingers itch to undo it. She wore some floaty thing, embroidered with daisies and violets on white muslin.

His pulse hadn't raced at the sight of a woman since his first season, when he'd learned he was far more likely to be the pursued rather than the pursuer. But when he saw Lady Mowbray, his heart performed an unaccustomed skip. He felt a sudden urge to go on his knees and thank her for rescuing him from a miserable marriage with a silly, giggling chit straight out of the schoolroom.

Pascal caught the hand she extended and bent over it. A less devious man might risk a kiss, but he played a subtle game. A game he'd started so often that it had begun to pall. London's handsomest man rarely failed when he set out after a woman.

Another surprise today. With Lady Mowbray, the game seemed intriguing and new.

"I'm astonished you can see me amongst all these floral tributes." It was an effort to keep the sourness from his tone.

She glanced around with a smile. "They're throughout the house."

"You made a triumph last night."

Pascal considered himself too jaded to find a

woman's blush charming. But the pink coloring Lady Mowbray's creamy skin beguiled him.

"They're not all for me. Lady Norwood's niece made a pleasing impression. And of course, Sally and Morwenna are lovely."

"They are. But the night belonged to you."

She tugged her hand free—he'd been in no hurry to release her—and fluttered her fingers in an unexpectedly dismissive gesture. One might imagine she wasn't used to compliments. "You're too kind. By the way, thank you for your lovely pink roses."

He dipped his head in a brief bow. "I'm glad you like them." He searched the room without seeing them. Were they somewhere else or, God forbid, had she thrown them out? "I called to see if you'd like to come driving. A lady who has made such a splash should confirm her conquest by gracing Hyde Park at the fashionable hour."

He'd swear the bewilderment in her eyes was real—he'd seen enough false modesty in his time to know the difference. "That's not until five o'clock."

"I hoped you'd give me a chance for some private conversation first. There's so much I want to know about you."

"Pascal, good afternoon." Sally appeared in the doorway and held out her hand.

He bowed over it politely, without any particular urge to lengthen the contact. "Sally, you're looking lovely as ever."

"Thank you." Her perceptive green gaze shifted between him and Lady Mowbray. "You've not long missed the crowd. We've had callers all afternoon. Amy has caught society's eye."

"Twaddle." Another of those damnably charming blushes. "Most of the callers were for Meg."

Sally leveled a stern glance on her. "No, most of them were for you." She paused. "Although I'm delighted that my niece has her admirers, too."

"I've invited Lady Mowbray for a run in my curricle." He'd deliberately left his call late to avoid tripping over every fop in London.

Sally subjected him to another of those assessing stares. He'd known her for years. They were the same age, and he'd danced with her at her first ball the year she married the fabulously wealthy Lord Norwood. "That would be an excellent idea. The approval of society's darling will do wonders for Amy's cachet."

While Amy looked daunted, Pascal gave an amused snort. "I'm not escorting the lady for the benefit of those other blockheads. I want to find out more about her."

Sally's eyes narrowed. She would know, even if Amy Mowbray didn't, that those words constituted a declaration of intent. He waited for her to comment, but she merely turned to Lady Mowbray. "I'll keep Lord Pascal company while you run upstairs and fetch your bonnet and pelisse."

When they were alone, Sally crossed to fill two

glasses of brandy. She passed him one, took a sip from hers, then fixed an uncompromising stare upon him. "Amy is my friend."

He arched his eyebrows, enjoying the unconventional sight of a woman drinking spirits. "Are you warning me away from her?"

Sally shrugged and wandered over to look out the window to where his groom held his fine bay horses. "No. But I'm saying if you hurt her, I'll feed your liver to my foxhounds."

"Ouch," he said mildly. "I'm inviting her for a drive. We're joining the fashionable throng in the park. She'll enjoy that."

"I'm sure she will. Didn't I hear a rumor that you were about to offer for the Veivers chit?"

"You know how inaccurate gossip can be," he said lightly, hiding a shudder.

"She's rich and pretty."

And as stupid as a bale of hay. In fact, in an intellectual contest, he'd back any bale of hay over Cissie Veivers. "So is Lady Mowbray."

"Just don't turn Amy's head."

He smiled. "Sally, you make a fine bulldog, protecting your charges. Your niece is only eighteen and needs you. Lady Mowbray is old enough to look after herself."

To his surprise, Sally didn't look convinced. In fact, this whole conversation was surprising. He was considered a catch. The estates might suffer a temporary cash flow problem, but the land was good, and his title was old and distinguished. And while he'd long ago become bored with praise for his looks, he knew he still set the ladies' hearts aflutter.

"Remember—foxhounds," she said darkly, as Lady Mowbray returned in a devilish stylish dark green pelisse and a military-style hat to match. His heart performed that strange somersault again. She wasn't pretty in the classic style, but by God, she was as bright and vivid as a sunrise.

"You and Sally looked very serious," Lady Mowbray said, as they rolled away from the front of the house. His groom was waiting for him back in Sally's kitchen —Pascal didn't want anyone overhearing this conversation.

"She was warning me to be careful with you." Deftly he angled the light carriage between two heavy drays threatening to block the road.

Annoyance flashed in her hazel eyes, turned them a rich gold-green. "Did she indeed? I'll have a word with her when I get home."

"She has a point. I have a reputation as a rake, and I'm famous for trifling with ladies' affections, then dropping them cold."

"I know about your reputation." She studied him with that direct, inquiring gaze he recalled from their dances last night. "All Silas's society friends are naughty men."

"Your brother isn't naughty anymore." Eight years

ago, Lord Stone had married a lovely widow, and he'd been blissfully happy ever since. Something about Amy Mowbray's company on this fine day made Pascal wonder if emulating him mightn't be a bad idea.

"Not in public, anyway."

"So you're not afraid of my intentions?"

Still she inspected him, as if she saw beneath his spectacular hide to the less than spectacular soul beneath. With most of his flirts, problems invariably arose once the lady discovered an average man lurked beneath his apollonian looks. They expected a prince, and instead got Gervaise Dacre, with all his faults.

Under Amy Mowbray's regard, he shifted uncomfortably. He had an awful suspicion she already guessed he wasn't a perfect knight.

The pause lengthened. "Lady Mowbray?"

A faint smile lifted one corner of her mouth. He bit back the impulse to kiss her. One day, he would. Not today. And not when he had to devote at least half his attention to negotiating London's bustling streets.

"You know, I'm not sure I am." Her smile lengthened. "Although I'm hurt you don't remember that we've already met."

The carriage's gentle rocking bumped her hip against his in a pleasing way. "You've been to London before?"

"I had a season before I married. But before that, you came to Woodley Park for the hunting. I had a horribly painful case of calf love for you when I was fourteen, my lord."

He racked his brains. He remembered visiting Lord Stone's beautiful Leicestershire estate on several occasions. He remembered Helena, Stone's dashing dark-haired sister, and Robert, tragically lost at sea a couple of years ago. "I should have noticed you."

She made a dismissive sound. "No, you shouldn't. Not really."

A glimmer of memory sparked. "You were the girl who talked farming at dinner."

Another blush. "I was an awful bore."

He laughed and shook his head. "You terrified the life out of me. I already didn't feel clever enough to be a guest in that house. Helena and Robert discussed mathematics. Silas was busy with his botanical specimens. And most intimidating of all, there was this young Minerva who knew all about new strains of wheat. I felt hopelessly shallow."

"We can be a bit overwhelming when we're together."

Pascal frowned, struggling to summon the details of those long ago house parties. "We danced together, didn't we?"

She looked sheepish. "Now I am surprised you've forgotten that. I bruised your toes most egregiously."

He gave a low laugh. "You didn't last night. You've been practicing."

A mysterious smile curved her lips. "I have."

It was his turn to study her and try to winkle out her secrets. Luckily they'd turned into the park so he was no longer at risk of killing someone, if he didn't pay attention to driving. "Make me a happy man, and tell me you're still carrying the willow for me."

"Don't be absurd." The blush intensified, and she looked away. "I've been married and widowed since then. My passing fancy for you ended nearly ten years ago."

"Pity," he said shortly. "Are you still interested in modern farming?"

Her expression turned wry. "If I say yes, does that mean you'll drop me from your list of dance partners?"

"No, I don't think it does," he said slowly. "I could listen to you talk about anything, even marrows and parsnips."

A dry laugh greeted what had been a sincere statement, damn it. "My lord, you'd better watch out. I might put that flummery to the test. There's a new variety of turnip coming out of the Low Countries that has me in alt. I can talk about it for hours."

He shook his head, enjoying her humor. Her crackling intelligence was devilish appealing. Especially after a month of Miss Veivers and her ilk. "I look forward to hearing about it."

"No, you don't."

Actually recent bad harvests had turned his mind to crop yields, if only out of self-interest. "So you were madly in love with me," he said in a considering tone.

"Quite madly." With exaggerated ardor, she batted her eyes at him.

"So who was the cad who stole you away from me?" He set the horses to a gentle amble, so he could concentrate on the woman beside him.

Regret shadowed her eyes to the color of light through a forest glade. He'd never met a woman with such an expressive face. "You're asking about my husband."

"Yes." He drew the carriage to a stop under a chestnut, coming back to life after a long winter. Pascal had an idea how that felt.

Admiration and social success had spoiled him. The ennui of the last few years was the inevitable result of never needing to strive for anything. In Amy Mowbray's company, ennui was the last thing he felt. Marrying this widow for her money promised to be a complete and undeserved delight.

She avoided his eyes and smoothed her dark green skirts over her knees. "How odd. We're already progressing beyond small talk."

"We are."

"I think...I think I'd rather talk about the weather."

"Really?"

He let the silence extend, until she turned troubled eyes up to meet his steady gaze. "We're strangers, my lord."

They were concealed from sight, unless someone followed the winding path behind them. He placed his hand on hers where it twisted the material of her skirts. Over the years, he'd explored every sensual pleasure, so touching Amy's hand should have no great significance. But when she didn't pull away, he felt a surge of anticipation completely out of kilter with the action's innocence.

"Nonsense. I've known you since you were fourteen."

"Even if you don't remember." She cast him an unimpressed glance under her thick fan of eyelashes. "And should we be holding hands in public?"

He smiled, unexpectedly enchanted. Last night, he'd liked her, and he'd found her attractive—what red-blooded man wouldn't? But today, every second changed the performance of duty into the pursuit of pleasure.

The world considered him a lucky sod. Right now, when fate offered him the chance to bed Amy Mowbray and at the same time, solve his financial woes, he was inclined to agree. He knew enough about women to recognize that, while she was far from won, she was intrigued. There was a catch to her breath, and the heaviness in those bright eyes betrayed sensual interest.

"There's nobody here but us."

"I'm well aware of that."

He looked around, as if checking for observers. "A man must seize his opportunity."

"Lord Pascal..." she said repressively, although the throb of excitement in her voice ruined the effect.

"Lady Mowbray." He tightened his hold on her hand, although she hadn't tried to pull away. On the narrow seat, her hip nestled warm against him.

Good intentions could go to blazes.

He leaned in and brushed his lips across hers. There was a fleeting sweetness, a huff of feminine outrage, the impression of softness. Then he drew back, astonished at how difficult it was to resist returning for a longer taste.

"Nice," he whispered.

The air shimmered with awareness, before she broke the thread twining between them with a soft laugh. "My goodness, you really are a rake. How exciting."

Curiosity lit her eyes, and her lush lips were still parted. Then and there, he decided that this pursuit was serious. Probably the most serious thing he'd ever attempt in his hedonistic, purposeless life. "Reformed rakes make the best husbands, I've been told."

Shock widened her eyes, banished the amusement. More shock than she'd demonstrated when he kissed her. Which was interesting.

"Husbands?"

He smiled self-confidently and turned his attention to the horses, flicking the reins to get them moving again. "I warned you I had intentions, Lady Mowbray."

CHAPTER THREE

*a*s the carriage rolled into motion, Amy was breathless, caught up in a dream, rushed along from event to event with no logic to link them. Her lips tingled after that brief kiss in a way they'd never tingled after her husband's rare kisses. Now the man she'd mooned after as a girl said he wanted to marry her.

She resisted the urge to pinch herself. When she was a dizzy adolescent, head over heels with her brother's picturesque friend, she'd imagined Pascal declaring his love. In her innocence, that had usually involved a rose garden, and a white horse, and endless yearning looks.

By the time she turned sixteen, she'd recognized those fantasies as mawkish and unrealistic. Heavens, if she'd thrown in a couple of unicorns and a troupe of dancing fairies, her dreams couldn't have been more unlikely to come true.

Since then, she hadn't entertained a single romantic thought. Until Lord Pascal had danced with her and revived the remnants of foolish girlhood that lingered under her practical manner.

She was too flustered to be tactful. Not that tact came naturally anyway. "We have nothing in common. The idea's ridiculous."

Instead of taking umbrage, he laughed with sardonic appreciation. "This is the first time I've discussed marriage with a lady. You could be a little kinder."

"I'm sorry." She'd noticed last night that for a man whose handsomeness was universally praised, he showed a refreshing lack of vanity. "You caught me by surprise."

"I hoped to avoid any misunderstandings about where my thoughts are leading." He still looked amused. "You're not an ingénue, Lady Mowbray."

The problem was that in most ways that counted, she was an ingénue. She realized that her hand still lay in his. The first time he'd touched her, her heart had turned cartwheels. It said something for how he'd distracted her today that she'd forgotten they held hands.

She slid her hand free and clenched it in her lap. "You're mocking me."

He frowned. "Not at all."

"Then why would you say such a nonsensical thing?"

He cast her a wry glance. "Kinder, please, Lady Mowbray."

"You'll have to forgive my manners." She sucked in an annoyed breath. "I'm not used to strangers wanting to marry me. I wondered if it was some peculiar London joke."

"You're a beautiful woman." He studied her with a puzzled expression. "You must have men after you all the time."

"Hundreds," she said drily and with perfect honesty. There was her farm manager, and her tenants, and her neighbors who, after initial reluctance to accept a woman's advice on farm matters, now clamored for her help.

She was startled when Lord Pascal accepted the answer at face value. "Exactly. So if I'm bowled over, why should you be surprised?"

"You're very direct." She hadn't expected that. His extraordinary looks deceived her into thinking this was a man who would woo a woman in rhyming couplets. "You're not at all as I imagined when I was fourteen."

His laugh held a hint of self-derision. "I'm a fairly basic fellow. Does that disappoint you?"

She thought back to the buffle-headed milksop her infatuation had constructed in her mind. "No."

He brightened. "So I've got a chance?"

She stifled a laugh. "No."

This close, there was no avoiding his substantial physicality. The arms clasping her in the waltz had been impressively muscled, and the body next to hers on this cursed small seat was hard and lithe. And warm as a coal fire.

His hands lay loose on his powerful thighs, the reins draped over them. Everything about him was perfect. The idea that he might want a harum-scarum ragamuffin like Amy Mowbray was outlandish.

But of course, thanks to Sally's efforts, she wasn't that ramshackle bumpkin anymore. At least on the outside. On the inside, she was still her plain, outspoken self. The knowledge that if Pascal had encountered her a month ago, he wouldn't have spared her a glance increased the feeling of unreality.

"Why?" he asked.

"In any true sense, we met last night. You know nothing about me."

"The best part of marriage is all the things you discover after the vows are spoken."

She shook her head and clasped her gloved hands in her lap. "You can't possibly mean that."

"Why not?" He seemed content to let the horses amble along through the dappled sunshine under the trees. "Anyway, I know more about you than you think."

"Oh?" She waited for some flippant reply. But his expression was serious as he studied her.

"You love your family, and you're loyal to your friends. You're very clever. You have a romantic streak, but you do your best to repress it. You consider yourself a sensible woman—and most of the time, that's true. You have a dry sense of humor, and the ability to mock yourself and the pomposity of others. How am I going?"

Some women might find it flattering that an attractive man paid such minute attention. Amy was uneasy. The woman he described was better than she was, but the resemblance was unmistakable. It wasn't her. But it was certainly a version of her.

"You make me sound as if I have no faults," she said gruffly.

His smile conveyed too much affection for a man who had only met her last night. "I make you sound like you're perfect for me. I saw immediately that you were something special. And I, my dear Lady Mowbray, am a connoisseur."

She stared back, both fascinated and appalled. "This is some sort of game."

"On my honor, it isn't." He flicked the reins at the horses to urge them to a trot. "I begin to suspect something else about you—you pretend to more confidence than you possess."

She cringed. Sally and Morwenna had both said the same thing. "What on earth makes you say that?"

"Your reaction to my proposal, for one thing."

"I'm very good at running my estate."

"Oh, I'm not saying you underestimate your brains or competence. But I'm beginning to wonder whether you realize how brilliantly you sparkled last night. Everyone admired you."

She sighed, as the carriage bumped across the grass. "That was because you made such a fuss about dancing with me. Every woman in that ballroom envied me."

"And every gentleman envied me. You may as well accept we make a fine pair."

She bit back a laugh, even as what he said seeped down through chronic self-doubt to settle in her bones. Perhaps Sally had performed a miracle, transforming the hardy thistle Amy Mowbray into a fragrant rose. "Which is no reason to seek a more permanent arrangement."

He shrugged, not shifting his gaze from the bays. The carriage emerged from the trees onto the lawns where the ton gathered to see and be seen. "I'm thirty years old. I've been out in society for more than ten years. I've pursued women, and women have pursued me. I've learned to tell the genuine jewels from the paste, literally and figuratively. You, Lady Mowbray, are a diamond. A man would be a fool to sit back while some other damned oaf picked you up and put you in his pocket."

With the presence of other people, the intensity between them receded to a bearable level. Even if Pascal was still talking tosh. On that secluded path, every word had wrapped around Amy like rope, until she feared she'd never escape.

Now she burst out laughing. "Lord Pascal, I appreciate your kindness. I wonder what you'd say if I took you at your word and had the banns called."

His wicked smile deflated her returning ease. "My dear Lady Mowbray, I'd say you've made me the happiest man in England."

Before she could protest, he was bowing to a handsome lady and her daughter who drew their carriage to a halt beside them. The ladies looked vaguely familiar. Amy's life in Leicestershire involved meeting the same people over and over. The onslaught of new faces last night had left her floundering.

What a bizarre world London was. Populous and bustling. Yet strangely intimate, so one encountered the next day the people one had met the night before. While she murmured polite responses to the lady's questions, her eyes roamed the stylish crowd. So many familiar faces, some she could even put a name to.

In the distance, she saw Sally driving a phaeton with Meg and Brandon beside her. She forced her attention back to Lady Compton-Browne and was shocked to catch flaring dislike in Miss Compton-Browne's eyes.

Amy summoned a smile, but the girl no longer looked at her, but at Lord Pascal. Her expression betrayed the misery of a dog drooling after a juicy bone placed high out of reach.

Ah.

Pascal made his excuses and rolled the carriage forward to greet more of his friends. That set the pattern for the next hour, and to Amy's surprise, she enjoyed herself. Nobody treated her like an interloper, or questioned her right to be with this superb man. She even found the confidence to face down the ladies' envious stares.

"You've made me a social success," she said wryly, when Pascal pulled the carriage up with a flourish before Sally's front steps.

"Nonsense. You did that yourself."

"Having you as my escort didn't hurt."

"It certainly didn't hurt your escort. He's had a thoroughly delightful couple of hours."

"So have I." To her relief, the heavy traffic on the way home had given him no opportunity to revive that troubling conversation about marriage. His boldness left her scared and unsettled and puzzled—and stupidly, dangerously tempted. For more kisses, above all. Some hitherto unrecognized feminine instinct insisted that if Pascal bent his mind to it, he could kiss her to heaven and back. "Thank you."

Sally's gleaming black door opened, and a footman ran down the stairs to hold the horses. Another appeared to assist Amy to alight, but retreated to stare stalwartly into space when Pascal shook his head.

"My pleasure. I'm glad the drive wasn't nearly the ordeal you expected."

She released a startled gasp of laughter. Perhaps he did know her better than she thought, after all. "Oh, dear, Sally would be disappointed. She tried so hard to teach me to pretend all of this is a mere doddle to my sophisticated self."

"You acquitted yourself beautifully, Lady Mowbray. I told you—I'm paying special attention."

Just like that, her earlier tumult returned. Her stomach knotted, and the moisture dried from her mouth. "Lord Pascal..."

He jumped down from the carriage to come around to offer one gloved hand. "Don't fret."

"Don't fret?" she whispered with sudden temper, but too conscious of the servants to give this arrogant, disturbing—gorgeous—man the set-down he deserved. "Of course I'm going to fret."

"Good," he said, still smiling as if she wasn't telling him off. His teeth were as perfect as the rest of him. Straight. White. And somehow predatory.

"What the devil do you mean by that?" She placed her hand in his and made a creditable descent from the carriage. Heat curled up from his fingers and settled in the pit of her stomach in a most disconcerting fashion. Except a woman would have to be dead not to find Pascal attractive. And however quiet Amy's life might have been in recent years, she was far from dead.

"When you fret, you'll be thinking of me."

"Not necessarily with fondness," she said grimly. The groom in his bright blue livery ran up the stairs from the kitchen, bowed to his employer, and settled in the seat at the back of the carriage.

Pascal laughed again. "Well, I'll be thinking of you—and fondly."

For a searing moment, his gaze focused on her lips, and she was transported back to those dazzling seconds when he'd kissed her. She hadn't scolded him nearly as severely as she should for that piece of daring. In fact, she had a horrid feeling she hadn't scolded him at all.

"You're engaged for Lady Bartlett's ball tonight?" he asked.

"Yes," she said, and realized he still held her hand. She had to stop doing this.

She pulled away, struggling to ignore a pang at the separation. She couldn't stand out in the street, holding hands with Lord Pascal as if they were sweethearts. The innocent description seemed incongruous for such a worldly man.

"Will you save me both waltzes?"

Her lips twitched. It was devilish difficult to cling to anger. Dear Lord, he was a master at these flirtatious games, while she was a mere novice. "No, I will not."

When he placed one of those elegant hands on his heart in a tragic gesture, she giggled. And Amy couldn't remember giggling since she'd been a silly chit under this very man's spell.

"Cruel beauty." His blue eyes—that was such an impossible color—sharpened. "One waltz."

"Very well."

"And the supper dance?"

"My lord—"

"Excellent." Another flashing smile as he caught her hand and bent over it. She braced for his lips on her glove, the way she'd await a blow. But the contact never came, although the way he squeezed her fingers set her giddy heart racing. "Until tonight."

He jumped into the curricle and waited as Amy went inside. Only her conscience knew how difficult it was not to look back and watch him drive away.

CHAPTER FOUR

*W*hen Amy walked into the house, Morwenna was writing a letter in the drawing room. "Amy, come and talk to me."

Amy took off her hat and coat and passed them to another of the ubiquitous footmen. Smoothing her flyaway hair, she went to join her sister-in-law, who had already put aside her pen and poured her a cup of tea. The room still looked like it held every flower in London, apart from one bouquet of pink roses which had escaped to take pride of place in her bedroom.

"Oh, you're an angel," she said gratefully, taking the cup.

"How was your drive with the notorious Lord Pascal? I do think he's the most heavenly looking man."

Amy found herself smiling, although she'd felt troubled and harried when she'd first come in. "Isn't he just? One itches to immortalize him in marble."

"His name was linked with Fenella's and Helena's, I gather. He clearly has an eye for a pretty girl. Watch yourself. He has a terrible reputation. One glance from those blue, blue eyes, and ladies go quite silly."

"I can imagine." Amy sipped the tea, considering what Morwenna said.

All her life, she'd heard gossip about Pascal. He'd not only flirted with Fenella and Helena, but with Caro, too. He seemed to have a penchant for widows. Was Amy Mowbray merely another in a long list?

"So did you?"

"Did I what?" Amy found a seat near the fire. The day had been warm for March, but as night drew in, a chill tinged the air.

"Did you go silly?"

For a long moment, she stared into the flames. When she answered, her tone was thoughtful. "You know, I think I might have."

Morwenna laughed in delight and rushed over to hug her, threatening to spill the tea. "I'm so glad."

"What are you glad about?" Sally asked, sweeping in and stripping off her driving gloves. Amy had been impressed with her friend's talent as a whip. Even from yards away, she'd seen that Sally handled a team of horses with aplomb.

Morwenna straightened and briefly Amy forgot her confusion about Pascal, and said a silent prayer of gratitude. Her sister-in-law looked pretty and happy and vital in a way she hadn't since the news of Robert's drowning. "Amy's made a conquest."

Sally strolled across to the tea tray. "Pascal? Good for you, Amy."

"I didn't say that," Amy said.

"He was very quick to call. And he was most attentive in the park. I thought poor little Miss Compton-Browne might burst into tears."

"I'm not up to his standard," Amy said, in no hurry to tell her friends of Pascal's marital intentions. She could hardly believe them, let alone expect anyone else to.

"Nonsense," Sally said, settling on the green-striped sofa and taking a bite of the delicate sugar biscuit she'd chosen to accompany her tea. "You need to accept that while you've hidden away like a little country mouse for most of your life, you're now a beautiful peacock, and all London knows it. Having Pascal, who is so generally admired, in pursuit only confirms your triumph."

"He's a dreadful flirt."

Sally's eyes sparkled. "Not so—he's a highly accomplished flirt. And there's absolutely no reason not to flirt back. When we came to London, it was on the clear understanding that we were to have fun."

"Are you suggesting an affair?" Morwenna asked. "How wicked."

Sally shrugged. "If Amy likes him, why not? She's a

widow, and a few discreet adventures won't spoil her chances of remarrying."

"I haven't thought about remarrying," she said slowly. Odd that marriage popped up in two conversations today.

"No reason you should. Except that you're young and pretty, and you might fall in love again."

Grimness tinged Amy's laugh. "There's no 'again' involved. I didn't love Wilfred. I married him to get my hands on his herd of prize shorthorns."

Sally gaped at her, then let out a peal of laughter. "Amy, you're priceless. I think in that case, it's well and truly time to seek a handsome lover."

"Who knows?" Morwenna sent Amy a sly glance. "Perhaps you'll find Lord Pascal more entertaining than a field full of fat Herefords."

"He's definitely prettier than a Hereford," Sally said.

"Sally, you have no idea how beautiful a fine cow can be," Amy said with perfect sincerity.

Morwenna threw up her hands. "Amy, you're utterly hopeless."

The Bartletts' ball was even more of a crush than the Raynors'. But Amy started to find her feet in this glamorous new world. Dancing twice with Lord Pascal last night and appearing in his company in Hyde Park had branded her, however unlikely, as a success. Within minutes of arrival, her dances were all claimed. Sally and Morwenna were equally in demand. It seemed the Dashing Widows lived up to their motto. Meg, too, was the center of a laughing, happy group of young people.

Amy danced with a string of handsome, elegant gentlemen who appeared to enjoy her company. She even managed an interesting discussion with Sir Godfrey Yelland about her recent article on cattle feed.

All was going as well as it possibly could. So why did the evening feel flat? Had she already moved from stark terror at the prospect of entering society to a disgust at the ostentation and overcrowding? With no period in between when she could bask in her unexpected popularity and admire this extravagant world. That seemed cursed unfair.

She'd saved Pascal two dances as he'd requested. Well, insisted. But so far, he was yet to make an appearance.

There were plenty of other candidates to dance with her, but she muffled a sigh as her latest partner returned her to Sally's side. She should have known Pascal's interest would fade. After all, London's handsomest man would hardly waste his time on a dressed-up rustic like Amy Mowbray.

But that didn't prevent a heavy lump of disappointment from settling in her stomach. The supper dance Pascal had asked her to keep came next.

"Don't look so downhearted, sweeting," a deep voice

murmured beside her. "Clearly it's time for the champagne cure."

The joy that gripped her was frightening. Still, Amy had the sense to compose her expression before she turned and curtsied. "Lord Pascal, good evening."

Her cool response amused him. "And good evening to you, Lady Mowbray." He bowed and passed her a glass of champagne. "Did you imagine I'd forgotten you?"

She put on an airy tone. "I wouldn't have lacked for a partner."

"I'm sure." He raised his glass in a silent toast. "Would you like to join the set, or take a walk outside? The Bartletts have put braziers on the terrace so their guests don't turn into icicles."

Wisdom dictated that after Pascal's declaration this afternoon, she'd be safer in a crowd. But the number of people crammed into the ballroom made Amy feel confined and suffocated.

And some small, untamed part of her wanted to be alone with Pascal. She thought his plan to marry her was ludicrous, but he was still the most exciting man she'd ever met. Even a brilliant occasion like the Bartletts' ball lost all flavor if he wasn't there.

When Sally had reminded her this afternoon of their pledge to become Dashing Widows, something inside Amy had broken free. She mightn't want to marry Lord Pascal. But by heaven, she meant to enjoy his attention while she had it.

She raised her chin and met those worldly blue eyes. "I would love a stroll, my lord."

The pleasure in his expression made her shiver. Mostly with anticipation, although enough of the old Amy persisted to add a dash of nervousness.

"Excellent." He presented his arm. "Shall we go?"

She caught Sally's eye as she headed toward the French doors. Her friend's smile brimmed with approval, before she turned to greet Mr. Harslett for the next dance.

"Are you enjoying the ball?" Pascal asked, as they stepped onto a terrace lit by torches and warmed, as promised, with braziers full of coals.

"Yes." Surprised, she realized it was true. Now that Pascal was here. Which made for a terrifying admission. "I'm sure you're so accustomed to London's whirl that one event becomes much like another. But since my marriage, I've led a very quiet life."

Pascal gave one of those mocking laughs that became familiar. "I'd be more convinced that your bucolic isolation chafed, if I didn't know how much you love it."

She cast him a quick smile and sipped her champagne. This was her second glass this evening. The first had been sour and flat. This glass, courtesy of Pascal, was just right. "You've discovered my shameful secret."

They wandered down the steps into the gardens. She caught glimpses of other couples snatching some air, away from the ballroom's stuffy heat, so she assumed this was perfectly acceptable behavior.

"It wasn't difficult once I worked out you were Stone's sister. You're the clever woman who wrote all those articles on animal husbandry. I should have known from the first, but then I never imagined I'd want to dance with an expert on hoof disease in beef cattle."

"You've read my pieces?" Amy asked, disconcerted.

"With interest. I'm trying the new farming methods on my estates, and my bailiff is a long-term admirer of your ideas."

"Th-thank you," she said, flustered.

There was enough light to reveal the fond smile he sent in her direction. "I do believe my appreciation of your work has thrown you into more of a spin than all the times I've told you you're beautiful."

Ridiculously, it was true. Perhaps because her agricultural experiments belonged to the real Amy Mowbray, whereas compliments he paid her looks were a tribute to Sally and her skilled modiste.

"I'd be glad to advise you," she said, then was grateful that the shadows hid her blush. What a nitwit she was. As if this sophisticated man wanted to talk agriculture at one of the biggest social events of the year. To hide her mortification, she gulped a mouthful of wine.

"I'd like that," he said with what sounded like enthusiasm. "Perhaps you'll come to Northumberland and see for yourself what needs to be done."

Her self-castigation melted away. Astonishing as it might be, he didn't dismiss her as hopelessly unsophisticated. She curled her hand around his arm more firmly. In thin evening gloves, her fingers were cold. More, she wanted to touch him.

The path he chose led away from the light. She noticed but didn't protest. The sinful hope arose that he might kiss her again. Properly this time. Wilfred hadn't been much for kissing, but she'd caught Silas and Helena in enough passionate embraces with their spouses to know that she had lots to discover.

Perhaps she'd discover it with Lord Pascal.

She edged nearer to him, partly because it was cold away from the braziers. In the distance, she could hear laughter and the sweet, silly tune for the dance. Closer, a woman murmured something in a husky voice, then fell silent.

Amy sipped her champagne, wondering if she could blame her uncharacteristic rashness on the wine. Her heart thumped like a drum, and her blood pumped slow and heavy like syrup. She'd never felt this way before. Such a giddy mixture of suspense and anticipation.

Desire.

Suddenly that seemed a sad confession. She'd been married for two years. She should have known desire.

Their steps slowed, came to a stop. They stood alone in a small glade with a sundial in the center. The moon was three-quarters full, illuminating shapes without detail. Very gently, Pascal set down his empty glass on the sundial. Then he took hers and set it beside his.

Amy swayed forward as with breathtaking assurance, his hand curved around her waist. He leaned in, blocking the moonlight, turning everything to dark mystery.

When his lips met hers, she sighed in wordless surrender.

CHAPTER FIVE

*P*ascal raised his hand to cradle Amy's cheek as their lips clung. Hers were soft and trembling like a young girl's, and her sigh expressed surprise as much as enjoyment.

Shock shuddered through him, pierced building pleasure. This lovely woman might have been married, but she kissed like a virgin.

Tenderness cut him, sharp as a sword. It was the most powerful emotion he'd ever known in a life devoted to selfish gratification. The pursuit of Lady Mowbray changed from an intriguing challenge and a pleasant way to answer his self-interest to something... else. Something outside the range of his experience. Or even his vocabulary to describe.

Slowly he pulled away, until the moonlight illuminated her unforgettable face. Her eyes were closed, and she looked transported to some higher realm.

After a kiss so chaste, he could almost have given it to an aunt.

Except that wasn't quite true. However sweet that kiss, it held the promise of sensual exploration to come. That kiss was a beginning, not an end in itself.

Amy opened her eyes, the hazel shadowy in the silvery darkness. Astonishing that such an innocent kiss set his heart racing with an excitement he hadn't felt in years. As if her innocence revived echoes of his, lost too long ago in a world that offered a presentable, aristocratic young man everything he wanted merely for the asking. Sometimes not even for that.

"That was...nice," she murmured.

He smiled, seeing her as so precious and fragile, for all her strength and cleverness. Some hitherto unrecognized chivalry in his soul made him want to cherish rather than conquer, coax rather than demand. "It was. Shall we do it again?"

"Yes, please," she said, like a child asking for another piece of birthday cake.

Pascal liked her lack of coyness. He was bored with the tired games where he was cast as the ruthless seducer, and the lady the helpless quarry. When the stark fact was on most occasions, women sought him out.

He'd become disgracefully lazy about his affairs. One lover became much like another.

Except this lover. Amy Mowbray wasn't like anyone else.

Hesitantly, she placed one hand on his shoulder, taking the initiative for the first time. His heart slammed against his ribs, and his breath jammed in his throat.

He tilted her face up, and this time he lingered over the kiss. Her scent mixed with the moonlit night and flooded his senses. Fresh. Female. Crushed flowers and a trace of musk. The air was cold, but her lips were warm. So warm.

Instead of enjoying an entertaining, but essentially forgettable interlude with an attractive woman, he let strategy sink to oblivion under a wave of unprecedented need. He leaned in, increasing the pressure, and her lips fluttered against his.

When his tongue swept along the closed seam, a tremor of response rippled through her. Unbelievably it seemed he needed to teach her how to kiss. Innocence had never held any particular appeal, but something about Amy's uncertainty touched him. When he nipped her full lower lip, she gave a soft cry.

He took immediate advantage, slipping his tongue inside to taste her. She was delicious. Hot, salty honey.

She recoiled at the invasion. "My lord..."

"Hush. Trust me," he whispered, and strangely he meant it. Tonight he wouldn't go beyond a few kisses. He played a longer game with Amy Mowbray than a mere night's pleasure, however incendiary. With every moment in her company, he was more satisfied with his choice of bride.

"What you did, it was odd."

"You'll come to like it."

She frowned, more in puzzlement than displeasure, he thought. "I'm not saying I didn't like it."

He laughed softly, enchanted anew. "Then let me show you more."

He brushed his lips across hers, and when she immediately parted, excitement sizzled through him. One hand splayed against the soft thickness of her hair. His other hand caught her waist and hauled her close, until those luscious breasts pressed into his chest.

This time when his tongue slid into her mouth, she greeted him with the slide of hers. His grip firmed as he deepened the exploration, relishing her sighs of enjoyment.

Dark heat descended to mesh him in delight. Desire throbbed through him, lured him to touch her body. The curve of waist and hip. The line of her flank. The soft swell of her breast.

When his palm brushed her pebbled nipple, she gasped and pulled away. Not far, but enough to wrench him back to reality. He and Amy weren't alone in a bedroom—more was the pity—but standing a few steps from one of the season's most glittering parties. And while society might forgive his rakish ways, it would look askance if a new arrival like Amy flouted propriety. At least publicly. Amy came from a respected family and had married well. Now she was a widow, the world would wink at a discreet affair or two.

Discretion being all.

As if to confirm how close scandal hovered, voices drifted in from the other side of the hedge. The distress on Amy's face made him wrap her in his arms and step soundlessly into the shadows.

The unseen couple were arguing about the gentleman's forthcoming trip to see his wife in Devon. Amy pressed close and clenched her hands in his coat. She was trembling. Fear of discovery? Or because he'd kissed her?

As she hid her face in his neck, he lashed her against his body. The unspoken trust in her action stabbed him with more of that poignant tenderness. Her nearness did nothing to soothe his unacceptable yen to ignore manners, morality, and the whole damn world, and run off with her somewhere private.

The interminable discussion continued, until Pascal wanted to throttle both participants. The voices were vaguely familiar, although it wasn't until he heard the fellow mention Barrow Hall that he identified Lord Bagshot. Which meant the woman protesting her lover's departure was Lady Compton-Browne, the lady with plans to become Pascal's mother-in-law.

The world Pascal inhabited was decadent, and hedonistic, and rife with hypocrisy. Amy seemed to come from somewhere purer and better. With a desperation that would have astonished him two days ago, he suddenly wanted to inhabit that world with her.

At last, the disputing lovers wandered off, fortunately without venturing into the haven that contained the sundial—and Lady Mowbray and Lord Pascal in a forbidden embrace.

Pascal stood holding tall, lissome Amy in his arms, marveling at how perfectly her body fitted against his. The music in the house had stopped, so he guessed that supper must have started.

He was so conscious of her, he felt the subtle shift of her muscles that signaled she was about to step away.

"That was my measure of excitement for the night," she murmured shakily, withdrawing a pace.

Where they stood, it was too dark to see her face, but he heard hard-won humor and lingering traces of fear. "I hope you mean the kissing."

"Of course I do," she said in a tone as dry as dust. "How could you think anything else?"

He caught her up and kissed her hard. When he released her, she regarded him breathlessly. "What was that for?"

"Luck." Her gallantry made his rusty heart cramp with admiration. He'd been caught before, doing what he shouldn't, and as a consequence, he'd dealt with enough hysterical women to last a lifetime. Amy's calm good sense made him want to marry her tomorrow.

"We should go in," she said, and he was pleased to hear the reluctance in her voice.

"We should." He took her gloved hand and drew her into the moonlight. "When can I see you again?"

"In about an hour. You asked me to save you a waltz."

He loved that she teased him, while he cursed the blasted rules that stopped him from tossing her over his shoulder and stealing her away to some isolated cave. "You know what I mean."

She shot him a wry look, clear even in the unreliable light. "I do indeed."

Pascal shrugged. "I want to be your lover. Why should I conceal it?"

He wanted to be more than that. But after those kisses, he was desperate to get her to himself. Anything more permanent could wait until he'd scratched this itch.

She had the most astonishing effect on him. He couldn't remember wanting a woman so much. Desire was a raging fever in his blood.

He'd never expected to be eager to bed the woman he married. Such a nice bonus that he was.

"And what would you think of me if I tumbled into your arms after a few kisses?"

"I'd think you were wonderful—and that you'd offered me a gift I'd treasure forever."

"That's all very well, but I don't know you." She held up her hand when he started to protest. "I know it was reckless to kiss you. I've clearly given you completely the wrong idea of my audacity."

He hid a smile. She'd felt like a virgin in his arms. He knew to his soul she hadn't kissed anyone since her husband's death. And if he was any judge of women—which he was—she'd shared damned few kisses when she was married.

Heat flooded him when he remembered how quickly she'd caught on. She had a rare talent that he intended to encourage. He tightened his grip on her hand. "Are you going to make me suffer for the sake of appearances?"

Her laugh was mocking. "A little suffering might do you good. You're far too sure of your attractions."

"And you're not confident enough of yours."

"Devil take you." She jerked free. He'd hit a nerve. "If I'm that appealing, you can jolly well work a bit harder to win me."

"I'm already mad for you."

She sighed. "I'm sure you've said that to every lady who has caught your fancy."

"I have. But that doesn't mean it's a lie."

Her expression critical, Amy surveyed him in the silvery light. "I imagine very few have said no."

To his shame, that was true. He couldn't remember the last lady to deny him. "A gentleman doesn't kiss and tell."

Her lips flattened. "Which means I'm right."

"What's in the past is past. I swear I'm a new man since I met you."

"Easily said."

Something in him would be disappointed if she accepted his extravagant claim, however true. What a fool he was to imagine she'd take him immediately. When he'd imagined he was on the verge of success, he'd been drunk on hope and kisses. "After those kisses, you can't send me away."

"You know," she said slowly, "I think I can."

Hell. Hell. Hell. He'd blundered. Somehow he'd ruined everything.

Black despair unlike anything he'd ever known in his privileged life crashed down. He finally met a woman he wanted as more than a temporary amusement, and now it seemed she didn't want him. "Amy…"

She arched her eyebrows and her voice was cool. "Amy, is it?"

He reached for her. Although what the deuce he'd do with her if he caught her, he had no idea. With half society within earshot, he couldn't tup her in Lady Bartlett's shrubbery. "Don't you want me?"

As she evaded him, he cringed to hear the stark need in his question. He was famous, some might say notorious, for taking his love affairs lightly. Two days in thrall to this unusual woman, and he hadn't a thought to call his own.

She took too long to answer. His gut tightened in suspense. And a vulnerability he refused to acknowledge.

He stepped closer. She retreated. He approached again.

She pulled back. "My lord, you're pushing me into the hedge."

"I'm sorry. I'm not acting like a gentleman." In fact, he behaved like an oaf. He had no right to bully her. The breath he sucked in was bitter with the taste of failure. Stepping away, he tried to tell himself that if she refused him, there were other women. "It's your right to end the acquaintance."

His schoolboy posturing had shoved her into the shadows. Perhaps even frightened her, which was the last thing he wanted. Damn him for a clumsy block-head. Damn these unaccustomed feelings that turned his usually practiced wooing into a complete mare's nest.

Pascal didn't expect his stiff pronouncement to evoke a low laugh. "I almost begin to believe you are sincere. You sound quite distraught, Pascal. Don't take on so, for heaven's sake. I haven't said no."

"You said you were sending me away." He hated his sulky tone.

"For tonight. At least until the waltz."

He frowned, trying to find cause for optimism, but not quite managing it. She sounded a little too busi-nesslike to be anywhere near yielding. "So you consent?"

"I consent to consider your offer."

"Then I must wait?"

Another laugh. He should resent that she found his

predicament so entertaining, but he was too damned grateful that he still had a chance.

"You could fill the time in between, trying to convince me that you're honest."

His pride kicked. "You want me to dance atten-dance on you?"

"I know. It's such an imposition." He winced at her sarcasm. She stepped into the moonlight again, and he read the stubbornness in her delicate jaw. "I hardly dare to imagine how I could even ask it."

Impossible wench. She set to torment him. "Send you flowers, and make polite calls, and take you to the opera?"

She folded her arms over her impressive bosom and regarded him steadily. "All of that sounds delightful."

His eyes narrowed on her. "You mean to put me through the hoops before you cede the game? I hadn't picked you as a woman who likes to torture a man."

Amy made a dismissive gesture. "I want to know you a little better before I abandon a life of perfect respectability to become your mistress."

"What about becoming my wife?"

This evening, he very deliberately hadn't mentioned his matrimonial intentions. In Hyde Park, she hadn't seemed too keen. He'd hoped a couple of kisses might make her more receptive.

He should have known better. Although at least she hadn't refused him outright.

"Becoming more familiar with you is even more important if we're contemplating a life together."

He liked the sound of that. He felt more cheerful, despite his impatience. "You want me to court you?"

"Yes."

He straightened. "I can do that." He paused. "What about kisses?"

She frowned thoughtfully, as if assessing a bullock's readiness for market. "I can't think when you kiss me."

He liked the sound of that even better. He smiled smugly. "Then clearly kisses must be allowed."

She cast him a repressive glance. "Clearly they mustn't."

He closed his eyes and groaned. "You're going to kill me."

"That would be a pity when you're so spectacular to look at. Every lady in London will weep at your funeral."

He glowered. "You think this is all a joke."

The teasing light left her eyes, and her expression turned austere. "Not at all. I just want to make sure *you* don't think it's a joke. I know it's hopelessly provincial of me, but if I give myself to a man, I want him to value my surrender."

Pascal could hardly blame her for mistrusting him. The irony was that he was more sincere than he'd ever been with a woman he wanted. Any promises he made to Amy, he meant.

He realized with a shock that while he'd launched

this pursuit to marry her money, now he'd willingly take her in her petticoat and beg on the high roads to keep her in fripperies.

After two damnable days.

The Good God knew what a wreck he'd be by the time he'd wooed her into taking him seriously. He'd be babbling nonsense and howling at the moon.

"You're enjoying this," he accused.

She nodded. "Most definitely. I came down from Leicestershire, afraid that society would laugh me back home again. Now I've got London's handsomest man begging for a moment of my time. Frankly, I'm ecstatic."

"I'm more than just a pretty face," he said resentfully, although his looks had brought him more benefits than disadvantages, so he had no right to quibble.

Until now, when the first woman he really wanted dismissed him as a lightweight.

The problem was he remained unconvinced he was anything else. Why demonstrate character, when a smile brought him everything he wanted?

But as he registered Amy's expression, he knew he'd have to dig deep and produce something more substantial than easy charm if he meant to win her.

"Prove it," she said implacably.

Fleetingly he contemplated giving up the chase. He could stroll away now and take on one of the little henwits he'd so dreaded marrying. Lucy Compton-

Browne or Cissie Veivers. Dash it, a proposal to either chit tomorrow, and his worries were over.

No mess. No fuss.

No joy.

It was too late. He was lost. Caught by a lovely face, and a brilliant mind, and a heart too fine for a careless brute like him. Which didn't mean he planned to retreat.

He faced the inescapable fact that he didn't want some ingénue with a fat dowry. He wanted Amy Mowbray, who might come with a fat dowry, but who also proved herself more complicated by the minute.

He sighed, resistance flowing away. She wanted to be courted. Then dash it all, he'd court her.

He bowed as if they were in a drawing room, instead of in the corner of a garden where he'd just been kissing her. "Lady Mowbray, it would give me the greatest pleasure if you'll come driving with me tomorrow afternoon."

She eyed him as if unsure of his candor. Then she curtsied briefly. "I'd be delighted, my lord."

"I'll call at three." It seemed an eon until then, but he could already see that a swift victory had been likely only in his fevered brain.

"Perfect."

"And I have a box for the opera that evening. Perhaps you, Lady Norwood and her niece would care to join me."

Her lips twitched. She'd guess how reluctantly he

included Sally and Meg in the invitation. "I'm not sure about tomorrow evening."

He sucked air through his teeth. "Damn it, Amy," he protested. "I'm trying."

To his surprise and gratification, she touched his cheek in silent reproof. Although the contact felt more like a caress than chiding. "I know you are, and I appreciate it. But I'll have to check what Sally has planned."

"Oh," he said sheepishly. He should have known that.

"Now, please take me back to the ballroom before they send out a search party."

The music had started again. He'd been too focused on Amy to notice. Luckily nobody had interrupted them. He made one last attempt to claim the masculine high ground. "Don't imagine you've got me on a string."

"Never," she said, too quickly to be convincing.

His voice hardened. "I'll make you pay for every day of frustration, once you've admitted I'm the only man for you."

"I'm quite terrified."

"Amy," he said warningly.

"Shaking in my dancing slippers."

"And one last thing. You're never to refer to me as the handsomest man in London again."

Her eyebrows rose with genuine puzzlement. "Don't you like it?"

"Not when you use that stupid nickname as an excuse to disparage my sincerity."

Her regard was thoughtful, but not censorious. "You know, I'm beginning to wonder if I've underestimated you, Lord Pascal."

He took her arm in a firm grip and cursed the fact that he couldn't kiss the insolence from her before he returned her to the crowded party. "I most ardently hope so, Lady Mowbray."

CHAPTER SIX

The next afternoon, Amy still couldn't believe that she'd had the temerity to lay down conditions to Pascal. He'd seemed even more incredulous. Clearly he wasn't used to his seductions meeting more than token resistance.

Given how astonishingly well he kissed, she couldn't blame him. She closed her eyes and relived those unforgettable moments in the moonlight. The heat. The pleasure. The hunger. The way everything outside the magical circle of his embrace ceased to matter.

"Are you all right?" he asked from beside her. As promised, he'd called to collect her in his carriage. Today, he'd taken her further afield, for a drive through Richmond Park nine miles outside London.

"Yes, perfectly," she lied. Telling him she already regretted the ban on kisses would only make trouble.

Trouble looked like a beautiful, golden-haired man. A man she had difficulty keeping at a distance, although she still retained enough common sense to recognize that she needed to know him better before risking heartbreak.

Because heartbreak was a definite possibility. As a girl, she'd longed for Pascal, the way a child dreamed of catching a falling star. But she had a nasty feeling that right now, she was on the verge of a painfully adult infatuation.

Pascal looked wonderful. When didn't he? The beaver hat was angled precisely right on his gilt hair, and his dark blue coat fit him to perfection and deepened the color of those beautiful eyes.

She tilted her bonneted head up to the pale spring sunshine. It was a glorious day, and now they were out of town, the rampant greenery mirrored the sensuality burgeoning inside her. The constant rub of Pascal's hip against hers was a reminder that last night she'd been lost in his arms.

"I love that you do that."

When she glanced at him, the lazy curve of his lips spurred her foolish heart into a headlong gallop. "What?"

"Turn your face to the sun. Most ladies are afraid of darkening their skin."

She laughed. "On my estate in the summer, you'd call me horribly weather-beaten. Sally's ordered me inside for the last few weeks to turn me pale and interesting."

"You're interesting anyway." Before the compliment had a chance to sink in, he went on. "Did Sally or Morwenna say anything about last night?"

Her lips twitched. "They enjoyed the ball and didn't lack for partners. Meg has a string of eligible admirers, which is excellent news."

"It is," he said. "Now stop teasing, and tell me what you three gossiped about over breakfast."

"They wanted to know where I'd disappeared to. I said a scandalous reprobate waylaid me."

"Do they approve?"

"Sally likes you. She's all in favor of a flirtation."

Satisfaction warmed his expression. "She's a good sort, Sally. And clearly full of wise advice. What about Morwenna?"

"Morwenna counseled caution."

"Sally's the one who knows London—and me."

"But Morwenna knows me."

"Sally gets my vote."

"There's a surprise."

Her sarcasm earned her a quelling glance. "Who got your vote?"

"Ah, that would be telling."

He gave a longsuffering sigh. "Did you tell them I kissed you?"

"No. I said we went for a walk in the garden and forgot the time."

She knew Sally hadn't believed her, and there had been sly amusement in her eyes when she'd waved them off on today's drive. Sally probably imagined they were kissing now.

Unfortunately, Pascal had been the complete gentleman. Amy hadn't been sure he'd stick to her rules, but so far, he'd only touched her to help her into the carriage. His obedience to her strictures should please her. Instead, it left her restless and longing.

And sharing this blasted narrow seat wasn't helping matters.

"If she swallowed that, she's not as sharp as I think she is. Did you tell her I want to marry you?"

"No."

"Why?"

Now, that was an excellent question, and one Amy wasn't able to answer. Was she still unconvinced that Lord Pascal wanted her? Were her feelings too turbulent and confused for mere words to express?

She didn't know. And tossing and turning for hours last night hadn't clarified matters. "Can we talk about something else? Tell me about your life."

A grunt of laughter escaped him. "I want you to stay awake."

"I did have a very late night." The embarrassing truth was that she was avid to find out about him. "Come, Pascal. I'm all ears."

He stared at the horses. "I was born."

"A good start."

He ignored her interjection. "The family estates are in Northumberland, up near the Scottish border."

"Brrr. So cold."

Again he ignored her. "I grew up. I scraped through a university degree. I entered society. I'd categorize my role since then as decorative but useless, although it's hard to regret much when I've so thoroughly enjoyed myself."

"And a host of women," she muttered.

He cast her a sideways glance, the brim of his hat shadowing his eyes. "Your jealousy only encourages my ambitions."

"Is that it?" she asked, when for a long while, the only sounds were the creak of the carriage and the rhythmic clop of the bays' hooves.

He turned the curricle off the road toward a string of ponds sparkling in the bright sunlight. The carriage bounced and jolted across the grass, and Amy fought the urge to cling to Pascal to keep her balance. Instead, she curled her gloved hand over the brass rail beside the seat. And wished it was a firm male arm.

"I'm what you see. Healthy. Unmarried. No unusual vices, if too many of the usual ones. Now tell me about you."

Her lips lengthened in disapproval. "Not yet. Do you have brothers and sisters?"

He pulled his team up on a grassy bank, set the brake, and leaped down. At their arrival, ducks and geese on the pond took noisy flight. "You really want to know?"

"I really want to know."

He came around the horses' heads and helped her down. "Very well."

"Go on," she said, and because he'd behaved all afternoon—something she had no right to resent—she let him tuck her hand into the crook of his arm. His warmth seeped into her, inevitably reminding her of kissing him last night. How contrary was she to want that again, when she was the one who forbade physical contact?

"No brothers and sisters." He started along the earthen path beside the water, matching his long stride to her shorter one. The fine weather meant the ground underfoot was mercifully dry. "My mother was a great beauty, but an inconstant wife. She soon decided Northumberland was too dull to be borne and fled back to London, while my father, who was a coun-tryman at heart, stayed at home with his sheep."

"Sheep can be wonderful company," Amy said, as she sifted what he said.

She was curious. His mother's desertion didn't seem to anger him. Instead, he spoke with fond tolerance, as if he knew she couldn't help herself. Very mature, but Amy couldn't imagine he'd felt that way as a child.

"So I discovered. I rattled around the chilly manor house with Papa, until I went to Harrow at eight, forsaking my ovine chums."

He spoke wryly, but this time, she wasn't fooled. "It must have been lonely."

Self-derision flattened his lips. "School was full of decent chaps. I was fine, once I got there."

She frowned. Did this mean that he loathed country life? If he did, he'd never be content with her. "What about your mother? What happened to her?"

"When she realized her son was almost as pretty as she was, she allowed me to come to London a few weeks a year. That was always great fun. But Papa didn't want his heir exposed to the feckless crowd my mother ran with."

Still moving at his side, Amy stared blindly across the pond to the trees beyond. Silly to grieve over that bleak, loveless childhood. Pascal had been torn between parents who were clearly a poor match.

Amy had already noted his complex relationship with his extraordinary looks. That ambivalence must have started when his mother used her son as a prop to her vanity. "What was your father like?"

"A good man. Much older than my mother. You've probably gathered it wasn't a harmonious union. They had little in common."

"Except you." Their quiet conversation had persuaded the birds it was safe to return to the ponds.

"Except me. He was kind in his fashion, although he had no real idea how to manage a child. I think we were both relieved when I went away to school. He died when I was twelve." The soft thud of Pascal's boots created a gentle counterpoint to this sad history.

"I can guess Harrow wasn't altogether easy." In wordless comfort, Amy squeezed his arm. Two brothers and numerous Nash cousins gave her an idea of what little savages boys could be. "You've forbidden any mention of your appearance, but I imagine a beautiful blond boy had trouble with bullies."

When he slowed to a stop, she slid her hand free and turned to face him. They stood near a reed bed where a warbler sang for a mate. The sweet music rang out across the cool spring air.

Pascal sent her an unreadable look. "I had the odd fight. I needed toughening up."

Amy didn't comment on what she knew must be a rank understatement. She was too busy trying to hide her appalled reaction to the revelations about his barren family life. He'd loathe her pity.

He looked like he had everything the world could give. Yet he'd lacked something as basic as a mother's love. He might still be a stranger, but his pain tore a jagged crack in her heart.

"Is your mother still alive?" It was an effort to steady her voice.

"She died fifteen years ago when her lover's yacht went down off the Isle of Wight."

"I'm sorry."

He shrugged. "She wasn't made for old age."

Not for the first time, the perfection of his features

operated as a mask concealing the real man. "That seems...cold."

His lips turned down, as he took her arm again and walked on. "When I was a child, I adored her and clamored for her attention. After I came home from London, I'd cry for a week. But she lost interest in me, once I stopped being small and appealing. Gangly, pimply adolescents tried her patience—and she abhorred people knowing she had a son approaching manhood. By the end, we were strangers."

He spoke carelessly, but by now, Amy knew better than to trust his pretended indifference. The vibrating tension in the arm under her fingers indicated that the hurt still cut deep.

For his sake, she made herself smile, even as she wanted to fling her arms around him and apologize on behalf of fate for that desolate upbringing. "I refuse to believe you were ever pimply or gangly. I'll wager you always looked like a prince. No wonder you devoted yourself to pleasure when you hit London. The ladies must have gone into a frenzy for you."

His laugh held a sour note. "You describe a dashed shallow cove."

"That's what you want me to believe, isn't it?"

He leveled that deep blue gaze upon her. "What I want you to believe is that I'll make an excellent lover and an even better husband."

The abrupt change struck a jarring note. She knew how reluctantly he'd spoken of his past, but now he had, she couldn't help seeing beyond this magnificent creature to the bereft little boy.

Although if she told him that, he'd run a hundred miles. Just when she started to think that she might like him to stay.

It was clear she'd wring no more confidences from him today. The uncompromising line of his jaw told her that he'd unveiled as much of his soul as he intended. "We've made an excellent start."

His face creased with familiar humor. "You sound like a schoolmistress marking my arithmetic."

"Arithmetic isn't the subject here, my lord. You are."

The path petered out at a weir, so they turned to retrace their steps. "That's a damned uncomfortable thought."

"It shouldn't be. And you passed with high marks. You haven't even tried to kiss me."

His smile was rueful. "I've thought about it."

So had she. Last night's kisses had been so delightful, she could barely resist asking for more. And that way lay madness and ruin.

He shot her a sideways look. "Are you going to let me escort you to the opera?"

"Yes."

"Perhaps in a dark opera box, I can persuade you to break a rule or two."

"Sally and Meg are coming, too. And I believe Meg has invited Sir Brandon Deerham."

Pascal's sigh was theatrical in its glumness. "You have a cruel streak."

Surreptitiously she studied him as they strolled along the path. He looked more resigned than angry. She knew she tested him, which was the whole point, really. "You must think I'm unhinged when it's perfectly clear we're...attracted."

Talking about his childhood, a pall had fallen over his brightness. She could see he felt much more comfortable with flirtatious nonsense. "We are?"

"Of course we are."

His eyes glinted. "That gives me hope."

She snorted. "As if you don't know how dazzling you are."

The brief cheerfulness faded. "Oh."

Curse it. She'd been doing such a fine job of restoring his spirits, but now she put her foot in it. When she'd promised not to.

"Not just because of your blasted looks," she said with a hint of impatience. "I like you. Or haven't you realized that yet?"

He stopped so abruptly that her hand slipped free. "You do?"

"If I didn't like you, I wouldn't consider your proposal," she said, puzzled that this seemed to be news.

"So you are considering it?"

"Yes," she admitted, then wondered if she confessed too much.

His gaze intensified. "Then let me take you to bed."

When she burst out laughing, he looked offended. "What's so funny?"

"You are. You need to court me for more than an afternoon."

"Why?" He spread his hands, the picture of masculine bewilderment. "You like me. I like you—very much. There's enough heat between us to melt Greenland. We owe nobody allegiance. Stop teasing me."

His indignant outburst frightened the ducks off the water once again. They took off in a flurry of quacking and splashing and flapping wings.

Amy shook her head, as some foolhardy part of her longed to say yes. "You make it sound so simple."

"It is simple. It's the inescapable imperative of desire."

"Which promises to become very complicated indeed."

He exhaled with frustration. "You want me. I want you. What else do we need to worry about?"

Her lips tightened. He was a clever man. He understood her qualms, even if he claimed he didn't. "For a start, I'm not sure I want to marry again. I came to London to keep Morwenna company, not to find a new husband."

He sliced the air with his hand. "Then be my lover."

She shook her head again. "I've never taken a lover."

"How long have you been widowed?"

"Five years."

"And no glimmer of temptation?"

After his honesty with her, when it was obvious he'd rather have his liver dug out with a pitchfork, she could hardly tell him it was none of his business. She dared to share the embarrassing truth. "I've never been tempted."

"To take a lover?"

"To want to do…that."

He looked shocked. She could hardly blame him. "But you said you once had a penchant for me."

She made a dismissive sound. "That was childish stuff. I doubt I thought much beyond dancing with you. You're…talking about a different world."

He looked thoughtful. "But what about your husband?"

"Wilfred was forty years older than me."

Good God, that was a whole lifetime. "He wasn't capable?" He sucked in an audible breath. "You're not saying you're a virgin?"

She was blushing. "No, I'm not a virgin."

"But you've never felt desire." Pascal spoke slowly, as if coming to terms with her confession.

"Don't you dare feel sorry for me." Which was ironic, considering how she'd wanted to smother him in compassion not long ago.

Anger lit Pascal's eyes to blue flame. "Did he hurt you?"

"No," she said, appalled that he should think that. "Of course not."

"There's no of course about it," Pascal said grimly, taking her hand. When she jumped, he gave an unamused laugh. "Don't worry. I won't try my luck. But this is important, and I don't want to be driving back to London and juggling horses and traffic while you tell me the whole story."

"I'm not sure I want to tell you the whole story," she said grumpily, resisting as he drew her toward a wooden bench beside the path.

"Too bad. If you can listen to me whine about my parents, you can give me chapter and verse on your disastrous marriage."

"You didn't whine. And my marriage wasn't disastrous."

"Convince me," he said in a mild tone. He placed his hands on her shoulders, pushing until she sat.

"Why should I?" she said in a sulky voice.

He sat beside her, stretching his powerful legs in front of him. "Because you insisted we get to know one another." His tone softened. "Tell me, Amy."

CHAPTER SEVEN

*P*ascal heard Amy sigh as she stared across the grass to the water. After what felt like a long time, she turned to him. "I was eighteen when I married Sir Wilfred Mowbray."

"And long over your *tendre* for that popinjay Gervaise Dacre."

Pascal hoped his gentle teasing would ease her strain. This sharing of confidences was a devilish uncomfortable pastime.

"Oh, that was ancient history by then."

"Did you love your husband?"

She still stared at the ponds, silvery in the fading light. "I loved his herd of Hereford cattle."

Pascal gave a low laugh. "Is that why you married him?"

"That's what I tell people." She fiddled with the yellow ribbons tying her pretty straw bonnet under her pointed chin. Amy wasn't a fidgety woman. It was one of the many things he liked about her. But he didn't need the evidence of her restlessness to see that she hated speaking of her marriage.

Was he cruel to make her continue? Satisfying idle curiosity?

Except he was desperate to understand her, which to his shame, was something he'd rarely said about a lover. Somewhere Amy had changed from a means to an end, however appealing, to someone he cared about.

"But it's not the whole truth?" He caught her hand and brought it down to rest in her lap.

"No. Not the whole truth," she said in a hollow tone. To his regret, she slid her hand free.

"Will you tell me?"

Grim humor flattened her lush lips. "I have a horrible feeling I just might."

"You can trust me, you know." He meant it.

She leveled a considering gaze on him, hazel eyes somber and piercingly intelligent. After a pause, she sighed again, and her slender shoulders slumped in mute acquiescence. "Growing up, I never had much interest in the things most girls like. Dresses and dances."

"No boys?"

She stared down into her lap. "Not the ones my age anyway. They seemed so trite and childish. Probably because the men I worked with on the estate had skills and purpose. I'd run Woodley Park since I was sixteen.

That suited everyone. Silas could pursue his botanical work, and I could try out my ideas for improving profitability."

"Most successfully, I gather." She couldn't have been much older than sixteen when she published her first article on animal husbandry. Even for the clever Nash family, she was a prodigy.

"Yes, I had some luck."

She was too modest, but he let it pass. "So what happened?"

"Silas got married."

"To Caro Beaumont." Pascal had fond memories of his brief flirtation with the lovely widow, but from the first, Silas Nash had been her choice. "Don't you like her?"

"Of course I do. She's a darling, and she's made him so happy," Amy said emphatically. "But they came back to live at Woodley Park."

"All that marital bliss made you feel de trop?"

"You understand." The restless hand began to pleat her dark green skirts.

"I can guess."

"Then not long afterward, Helena married Lord West. They didn't live with us, but they visited. Often." She spoke the last word as if she accused them of murder.

A huff of sympathetic amusement escaped Pascal. "Even more wedded bliss?"

She cast him a grateful glance. "Exactly. And Robert

was away in the navy. Don't misunderstand. I was—I am—delighted for my brother and sister. They both deserve their happy endings, especially Helena, whose first husband was that swine Lord Crewe."

"But you were on the outside—and worse, with the master in residence, you no longer had free rein with the estate."

"Yes," she said, and this time, when he took her hand, she curled her gloved fingers around his.

"Enter Sir Wilfred Mowbray."

"Actually Wilfred had always been there. He was a neighbor, and he taught me many things I later tried at Woodley. He was a brilliant farmer, a real pioneer." Her voice expressed genuine admiration.

"Gad, that would set any young girl's heart fluttering."

His sarcasm raised a faint smile. "This young girl, anyway. Everyone thought Wilfred was a lifelong bachelor, but when he proposed and promised that together we'd build the finest herd of beef cattle in England, it seemed the ideal solution. I'd have a purpose and a home of my own—and Silas and Caro could settle into Woodley without my interference."

The bench was deuced hard on his arse, but Pascal didn't dare move and risk the flow of confidences. "Convenient all round."

Amy cast him a doubtful look. "I'm sure that all this strikes you as extremely banal."

He shook his head. This glimpse into what made

her such a remarkable woman was fascinating. "No. But I think you deserved better than you got, even throwing the prize cattle into the mix. You don't mention love."

Astonishment widened her eyes. "I didn't know you were a romantic, Pascal."

His heart leaped when she used the familiar name without appending the formal title. He'd buy her a county full of damned Herefords if she called him Gervaise.

"I didn't either. What a discovery," he said calmly, wondering what she'd say if he confessed that she'd made him so. "Don't tell anyone."

"I promise," she said with a laugh.

"A girl should be giddy with happiness when she gets married, especially a pretty chit like you. Your engagement sounds like a business contract."

She shrugged, unoffended. "But that's what it was. Wilfred and I were friends. Good friends. I hoped that was enough to go on with."

When she tried to pull away, Pascal held onto her hand. "No passion?"

"No passion. You're the first man to…" She broke off, watching the water birds scooting about the ponds.

"Go on."

"No, not now."

Of course she didn't need to explain. The first time he kissed her, he'd recognized her lack of experience.

And her fervent response. "So the wedding night wasn't full of fireworks?"

Amy bent so her bonnet hid her face. "I can't talk about that."

Pascal smiled down at her. "Don't stop now, when you're getting to the good stuff."

She lifted her head, eyes sparking green with anger. "You're very good at wheedling confidences out of people. I've never discussed this with anyone."

He'd wager that was true, given the way she forced out every word. "I'm guessing Wilfred did his duty, but neither of you fell under pleasure's spell."

"Wilfred wasn't much interested," she said, then continued in a whisper. "Neither was I."

Hell. What a bloody tragic waste. Pascal swore that when he got Amy into bed—and surely that was only a matter of time—he'd make up for all the arid years. "Poor sod."

She frowned. "I told you not to feel sorry for me."

"I'm talking about Wilfred. He had a gorgeous young bride with fire in her blood, and he didn't know enough to take advantage of his extraordinary luck."

"I'm sure he'd never been interested." Her voice was so low that Pascal had to lean closer to hear. "He told me he was an innocent, too, when we married."

And no doubt once the long-delayed occasion arrived to prove his manhood, he made a complete shambles of the act. "No wonder you're so skittish."

Amy cast him a displeased glance. "I'm not skittish."

His silence spoke volumes, and eventually she sighed. "Well, perhaps a little."

"Things with Wilfred didn't improve?"

She looked less hunted. "We did marvelous work on his herd."

He folded his arms. "You're avoiding the question."

"Can you blame me?" A flush marked her cheeks. Through her awkward recital, her color had come and gone. Pascal admired her bravery in telling him even as much as she did. He could see it was an ordeal.

"No. But I need to know who you are."

A line appeared between her marked brown eyebrows. "That's a powerful thing for a man to say to a woman. I hope you mean it."

"I do." It was a vow, whether she acknowledged it or not.

Around them, the day drew to a close. Rooks cawed monotonously from the trees behind him, and the starlings flew in to set up their twilight racket.

She sighed and stiffened her back, gathering courage to finish the story. "His attentions weren't… onerous. And when his health began to fail, we had other things to worry about."

Sadder and sadder. "That must have been difficult."

"It was." Her relief at shifting the discussion away from the bedroom was palpable. "I was very fond of Wilfred. He taught me a lot."

"And of course you still had your cattle."

"Don't mock me," she snapped, ripping her hand from under his.

"I'm not." Pascal desperately wanted to kiss her. No, he desperately wanted to whisk her away to Richmond's best inn, haul her into a room, and show her the joy two people could create out of lust and liking.

But he'd promised to behave, damn it. Although after hearing about her marriage, he took a kinder view of this enforced courtship. She deserved a wooing. Hell, she deserved a lover patient enough to persuade her into surrender. Then patient enough to show her just what she'd missed.

She rose, and he flinched when he saw her brush away a surreptitious tear.

"I'm sorry. I've stirred unhappy memories." He stood, too, but she extended a hand to deter his approach.

"I'm fine." Emotion thickened her voice.

"I don't regret asking you about Wilfred," he said softly. "But I regret upsetting you."

She fumbled in the pocket of her figure-hugging green pelisse and produced a white lace handkerchief. "I couldn't let you think my marriage was a disaster."

As far as he could tell, it hadn't been much else, but Pascal had the wisdom to keep that opinion to himself. "Wilfred was clearly a good man."

Which was true, too. A fumbling dunderhead when it came to his wife, but that wasn't the full measure of the fellow.

As reward for his discretion, he received a grateful, if shaky smile. "He was."

She'd mourned Mowbray, if only as a colleague. However unworthy the thought, Pascal was grateful she'd never loved before.

Did that mean he wanted her to love him?

Shock held him transfixed as he examined the question. Over the years, many women had professed to love him, starting with his flighty mother. A few at least must have meant it. The mawkish emotion had always proven a poisonous gift, laced with demands and tears, and the inevitable acrimony when the woman realized Pascal was incapable of loving her back.

But when he imagined Amy Mowbray loving him, that trapped, suffocated feeling was absent.

How…unexpected.

He extended his hand. "We should go back. As it is, it will be dark when we return."

She sucked in a shuddering breath, wiped her eyes again, and put away her handkerchief. To his relief, she took his hand, although she still looked unhappy. "Sally will think we've eloped."

He didn't express his approval of that idea, however much he liked it. Only a heartless villain would badger her about marriage, when she remained so heartbreakingly fragile. "Not her. She'll just think I conspired to keep you out late."

Amy managed another faint smile. "I haven't been much fun this afternoon."

He tucked her hand back into the crook of his elbow. As they walked toward his carriage, the shadows lengthened around them. A breeze promised a chilly trip back to London. "It doesn't always have to be high jinks and champagne."

She moved closer into the shelter of his body. He hoped not just because the air cooled. "Thank you for telling me about your parents."

"It wasn't a pleasure."

She gave a husky laugh. "I know exactly how you feel."

"After today, you can never call me a stranger again," he said gently.

"No," she said, and for the life of him, he couldn't tell whether that change left her pleased or dismayed.

CHAPTER EIGHT

*F*or two weeks, Pascal kept to his word and wooed Amy as he'd promised. If courtship was a new experience for her, it was no less so for him. He soon realized quite how careless he'd been with his previous amours. On the rare occasions when a woman denied him, he might devote a day or two to the chase. Should the effort prove too taxing, he'd shift his focus to someone else.

Now he looked back on all those years of pleasurable, but meaningless encounters, and couldn't help feeling they reflected poorly on him. A man shouldn't find it easy to shrug his shoulders and replace one woman with another. Somewhere a lover or two should have touched his heart.

But they never had.

Until now. Until he met a clever, skittish widow with a cloud of tawny hair and eyes that flashed

between green and gold. At thirty, he was late to his
first true affair of the heart, and the experience left him
floundering.

Not least because, instead of running into his arms,
Amy became increasingly distant. The flirtation that
started with kisses and confidences became less intimate each day. It was a damned backward way to win a
bride.

There were no more passionate interludes in the
moonlight, no more shared secrets. Several times, he'd
tried to broach her defenses, but she proved adept at
keeping him out. The irony was that when all his
previous lovers had sought to build emotional close-
ness, he'd maintained his detachment.

Now Pascal was the one to want more than a
woman was prepared to give.

He'd wager what little money he had that the gods
were laughing their heads off at him.

Most days, he drove Amy in the park. At the balls
they attended, she always granted him two dances,
including a waltz. They went to the opera, the theatre,
museums, picnics, musicales, breakfasts, balls. Society
began to treat them as a couple, and the clodpolls he
called friends snickered to see the former libertine
under the widow's spell. The world awaited news of a
wedding for the elusive Lord Pascal and the charming
Lady Mowbray.

Pascal wondered if it waited in vain. Which added
to the comedy, given that for the last ten years, he'd had

his choice of bride. Now he wanted to marry a lady, yet he couldn't pin her down for a definite answer.

In the beginning, he'd assumed Amy was all but his, and this game they played moved toward a fixed end. But as day followed discouraging day, his prize edged further out of reach.

Tonight, he waltzed with Amy at the Oldhams' ball. The music was lovely. The crowd was elegant. He had the woman he wanted in his arms. He should be in alt.

He wasn't.

She smiled up at him. But she'd also smiled up at every other partner with exactly the same delight and interest. Damn it, couldn't she see that he was special?

"Thank you for those beautiful red roses."

He hid a wince at her tone. Amy sounded polite, rather than enthusiastic.

Every day since he'd met her, he'd sent her a bouquet. "Too many flowers?"

"There's no such thing."

"And you've enjoyed the bonbons?"

"Delicious."

He sensed he was missing something. "You returned the diamond bracelet I gave you last week."

Her glance was disapproving. "That was a totally inappropriate gift for this stage of our acquaintance."

He still had the bracelet tucked away in the drawer of his desk. He hoped the day would soon arrive when it was no longer inappropriate—because Amy had stooped to some inappropriateness of her own. But that day wasn't now. Sometimes he gloomily wondered whether the day would ever arrive.

"It's a highly respectable gift. The bracelet belonged to my grandmother."

How he'd love to shower Amy with jewelry. Emeralds set in gold to match her changeable eyes. Pearls to shine white against her creamy skin. Rubies to symbolize this passion that never gave him a moment's rest.

But when he'd set out to buy her something sparkly from Rundell, Bridge & Rundell, his usually cooperative conscience had shrieked. The amount he spent on a pretty bauble would pay to reroof half the cottages on his estate.

"It was lovely." He caught a momentary softening at the mention of his grandmother, before she firmed that delicate jaw in a regrettably familiar fashion. "But you know I couldn't accept it."

"You can't blame a man for trying," he said ruefully. "That's why I went back to flowers and bonbons."

"And lovely they've been."

He frowned. "You don't sound as if you like them."

Her expression thoughtful, she stared over his shoulder as he twirled her around the floor in time to the lilting music. "I said I do."

"But?"

She gave a heavy sigh that he felt as much as heard. "It's just…"

When he didn't fill the silence, she reluctantly went

on. "It's just I can't help feeling that I'm in receipt of your standard mistress-catching set."

What the devil? He was torn between offense and laughter. "My standard mistress-catching set?"

"Oh, you know what I mean."

Unfortunately he had a fair idea, and he had to admit her accusation was justified. A little. "Tell me."

Another of those heavy sighs. "You decide to seduce a woman, so you bombard her with flowers and delicacies and gewgaws, the way you always do."

"But I mean it when I give you presents," he said, cringing at how weak that sounded.

She looked unimpressed. "I'm sure you meant it with the others—or at least you intended them to think so. Tell me, Pascal, have you ever offered anything except flowers and delicacies and gewgaws to a woman you want?"

He frowned, loathing how right she was. "Not since I came to London. There was a milkmaid I fell madly in love with when I was twelve. I gave her my best fishing rod."

She smiled dutifully, and he loathed that, too. "I hope she caught a trout or two, and you shared a romantic outdoor dinner."

"No, the faithless chit kept the fishing rod, while throwing me over for the plowboy. Since then, I've stuck to the usual tributes." He struggled to maintain his light tone. "Although if the battle looks lost, I've been known to produce a puppy. You'd be astonished how much sin a puppy can inspire."

Amy gave a short laugh, half-shocked. "You're a terrible man."

He whirled her around to avoid bumping into Sir Charles Kinglake and Sally. "You know that."

"I do." She paused. "I like puppies, but I really can't take one on, when Sally's putting me up."

"Pity." He'd already considered and dismissed including a kitten or a dog in the avalanche of pretty gifts. "So no more flowers?"

"I didn't say that."

"But you'd like me to put a little more imagination into my wooing?"

"I'd like to feel that you're trying to win Amy Mowbray, not some generic woman lined up to become your hundredth mistress."

Even as secretly he squirmed, he shot her a straight look. It was hell being in thrall to a clever woman. "I'm not quite up to three figures."

Something that might have been jealousy flashed in her eyes. That pleased him, even as he wondered what the deuce would convince her that she was unique in his existence. "Mind you, I have high hopes that a certain widow from Leicestershire will bring my total up."

Her lips flattened, and her tone turned arid. "You'll have to work a little harder, then."

This discussion had been dashed uncomfortable,

partly because she was right about his laziness, much as he didn't want to admit it. Now amusement won out over hurt pride.

"There's my schoolmistress again." To his regret, the waltz ended. Pascal held onto her until the last possible second. This damned vexatious courtship offered few enough opportunities to touch her. "It seems my arithmetic may need improvement after all."

Without shifting from his grasp, Amy narrowed her eyes on him. "It does, if you want one and one to make two, my lord."

Amy sat beside Pascal as his curricle negotiated the narrow country lanes. On this cloudy, but dry day, they were well into Surrey. They'd passed through Epsom half an hour ago. "This seems a long way to go for a picnic, my lord."

He didn't shift his attention from the horses, but the corners of the firm mouth deepened, as if her remark aroused some secret amusement. "I'm very fussy about where I eat."

They'd left London before ten, and he'd told Sally that they'd be back late. Amy might suspect some nefarious purpose—she hadn't missed his increasing frustration with her rules—if a groom hadn't accompanied them.

Usually when they went driving, Pascal left the boy

at Sally's. This adherence to propriety hinted that something unusual lay ahead.

Amy just wished she knew what the devil it was.

They hit a deep hole among all the other ruts, and she clutched his arm for balance. Then she made herself let go, much as she'd rather cling to him.

This decorous courtship tested her patience, too, and several times she'd wondered if she pushed him too far, and he'd look elsewhere for a mistress. But she had to give him credit. For more than two weeks, he'd been the perfect suitor.

"Are you still there, George?" Pascal asked, checking with the boy at the rear of the carriage.

"Aye, your lordship," the young groom said breathlessly. "These roads are a bit rum."

"They are indeed, my lad."

Amy had already noticed Pascal's easy manner with George. She liked that he wasn't highhanded with his servants. The problem was that she liked far too much about Gervaise Dacre, Earl Pascal. Her resistance grew ever more threadbare, yet she still wasn't sure she wanted to risk an affair.

It was an effort to maintain her sardonic tone. "You should have told me you planned dinner rather than luncheon, and I'd have had an extra sausage for breakfast."

This time he did look at her, the blue eyes suspiciously innocent. "If there's one thing our delightful acquaintance has taught me, Lady Mowbray, it's that patience is a virtue."

She gritted her teeth, as the curricle turned between two stone gateposts and bowled along a drive considerably smoother than the roads they'd taken to get here. "Where are we?"

A beautiful park extended on either side, with artfully placed follies and bridges. In the distance, she saw a lake, with just beyond, a magnificent Portland stone country house, built in last century's style.

"Didn't I say we were visiting a friend of mine? I'm sure I did."

Dear heaven, he could be irritating. "I'm sure you didn't."

"Oh, well, we're here now." With a flourish, he pulled up on the circular drive in front of the impressive double staircase. As a groom darted out to hold the horses, a familiar figure emerged from the house and ran down the steps with a vigor belied by his sixty-odd years.

"Welcome, welcome, Pascal and Lady Mowbray." Sir Godfrey Yelland smiled broadly and strode toward the curricle, where Pascal had leaped down and now helped Amy to descend. "My lady, I've been so looking forward to showing you my herd and hearing your opinions on my methods to increase milk yield. Ever since we danced together at the Bartletts', I've been thinking of what you said about changing my stock feed."

"Sir Godfrey." Goodness gracious, he wasn't who she'd expected to see.

"Yelland, so kind of you to allow us to visit," Pascal said.

"Not at all. Not at all. Was glad you asked to come. Privilege to have the famous Lady Mowbray here. I'm sure you're famished after the drive from London. I thought we'd have a meal, while I describe some of my experiments. Then we can spend the afternoon outside. The weather looks like it will hold."

"That sounds...that sounds delightful," she stammered, releasing Pascal's hand. "Although my expertise is in beef cattle, not dairying."

"When Pascal said you wanted to see my place, I was in alt. I'll take note of anything you say." Ignoring Pascal, he took her arm and marched her toward the steps.

"You're too kind, Sir Godfrey," she said unsteadily.

Before Yelland whisked her inside, Amy hung back at the top of the stairs to cast Pascal a grateful smile. An afternoon of tramping around Sir Godfrey's muddy fields was the best present anyone could give her, better by far than a wagonload of hothouse flowers.

Before she could put her thanks into words, Sir Godfrey bustled her through the imposing doors. "Now, you were saying you know about this new turnip from Zeeland."

CHAPTER NINE

*P*ascal had hoped that the hugely successful visit to Sir Godfrey Yelland would soften Amy's attitude. Possibly even win the war. Although her transparent pleasure in wandering around the baronet's lush fields and discussing the finer points of cattle management had almost been reward enough.

Perhaps Pascal wasn't quite the selfish sod he'd always considered himself. Or perhaps Amy made him a better man.

Which wouldn't stop him taking her to bed and proving himself very bad indeed, when she at last decided he'd done his time in purgatory.

He was still in purgatory. All those damned dairy cows hadn't worked their obscure magic. However fulsomely grateful Amy had been in the week since then, she still wouldn't permit him to kiss her. Let alone do anything more.

She was a stalwart opponent, his Amy. If he wasn't in such a lather to have her, he'd admire her determination. As it was, he wasn't far off banging his head against a brick wall, so he had something else to think about, apart from this endless sexual craving.

Tonight, they were in his box at the Theatre Royal, watching a comedy that was all the rage, some asinine nonsense about bandits in the Apennines. Pascal had paid attention to the first five minutes, then lapsed into his usual pastime these days, brooding over the woman who proved his torment and his delight. The lovely creature with a heart of ice, who sat beside him, giving every sign of enjoying the inanities on the stage.

Except she didn't have a heart of ice. She just didn't feel any particular warmth toward one Gervaise Dacre.

When they'd first met, he'd have bet his hope of heaven on the fact that she found him irresistibly attractive. Now he wasn't even sure of that anymore, devil take her.

What if, after all his restraint, she wouldn't have him? He reached a point where no other woman would do, but romantic yearnings couldn't restore his estates. He'd manage without marrying money, he supposed, but it meant economies, not only for him, but for the tenants. He was dashed reluctant to take that path. Over the years, he'd done bugger all to make his late father proud, but he'd always tried his best to be a good landlord.

Before the last scene of the play, there was a short

break. A backdrop descended, and the orchestra played popular tunes in a futile attempt to cover the thumps and bumps coming from the stage. Meg and Sally and Meg's new suitor, Sir Charles Kinglake, retreated to the rear of the box for a chat. Pascal waited for Amy to rise and join them, but she remained where she was.

"You're quiet tonight, my lord," she murmured. "Aren't you enjoying the play?"

Blast the play. He'd happily consign the play to Hades, and this buffle-headed audience with it. But he'd promised to act the perfect gentleman, so he battened down his frustration and responded evenly, if not politely. "I've never seen such twaddle in my life."

She laughed. He loved her laugh. His wayward heart always skipped a beat when he heard the husky catch in that low chuckle. Even now when he was utterly wretched. "It's silly, but funny. I thought you might like it. You didn't much take to 'Othello' last week."

He didn't much remember "Othello." As he had tonight, he'd spent most of the evening ruminating on his lack of success with a pretty widow. "That was twaddle, too."

"Would you like to go home?"

He brightened. That sounded like an offer to join him in his carriage. She joined him in his carriage most days, but right now it was dark, and who knew what liberties he could take between Drury Lane and Half Moon Street? Especially if they detoured via Edinburgh. "Would you?"

The shake of her head made his cheerfulness plummet. One of the worst parts of his plight was the way she sent his emotions flying to the sky or sinking to the depths.

"No, I'm enjoying the play. But I'm sure Sir Charles can take me home."

Over his dead body. "It's nearly finished anyway," Pascal said in a sulky voice, before he remembered he meant to be gracious and charming, so she allowed him into her bed.

During these last weeks of pretending he wasn't starving for her, he'd become a dab hand at dissembling. In fact, his acting was a damned sight better than anything he saw tonight.

"Are you going to the Lewis musicale tomorrow?" she asked.

"Are you?" Another chance for her to keep him at arm's length. How could he bear it? Blindly he stared at the insipid painting hiding the stage.

"Yes. Cavallini is singing, and everyone says she's marvelous."

More blasted twaddle. "Then I'm going, too."

"Sally's holding a small dinner at Half Moon Street before it starts. She'd love you to come."

He focused burning eyes on Amy. "And what about you? Would you love me to be there?"

When they'd first met, he'd had little trouble interpreting her expressions, but with every day, she became more of a mystery. He'd decided long ago that love turned a man's brains to porridge. "Of course."

"Of course," he muttered and turned back to watch as the painting rose to reveal more damned mountains. The whole bloody play had been about mountains. What was the point of moving the scenery at all?

The orchestra finished scratching away, and the noisy nitwits reappeared to play out this tosh. Pascal was vaguely aware of Sally, Meg, and Sir Charles taking their seats.

He could go home. Amy probably wouldn't mind if he left. But what was the point of retreating? The devil of it was that he was as miserable away from her as he was with her.

About ten minutes later, Amy leaned closer. "Stop sighing. You sound like an overridden horse."

Despite his morose mood, he couldn't contain a smile. "It's worse than 'Othello.'"

To his astonishment, she reached across and squeezed his arm. The gesture was friendly rather than seductive, but it still went a long way toward calming his roiling unhappiness. "It will soon be over."

If only she meant his wait for her. "I hope so."

He waited in suspense for her to pull away. She hadn't touched him in weeks, apart from sanctioned contact when she stepped into a carriage or danced with him.

"Thank you," she whispered, after a reverberant pause.

What a surprise. Pleased astonishment flooded him. He didn't need to ask what she thanked him for. It seemed that she'd noticed his efforts to woo her and appreciated them.

Even after she withdrew her hand, warmth lingered. Unexpectedly a few of the silly jokes on the stage turned out to be funny enough to raise a laugh.

"Goodnight, Aunt Sally," Meg said. Amy watched the girl bend to kiss her aunt's cheek. "It's been a lovely evening."

They were in Sally's sitting room, and it was late, well past midnight. After the play, Sir Charles had arranged supper at his fine house on Berkeley Square.

"Yes, it has," Sally said. "Sleep tight, and dream of handsome gentlemen."

Amy caught a hint of slyness in Meg's glance. What was the chit up to? So far this season, she'd behaved perfectly. But there was no mistaking the mischief in those dancing blue eyes.

"Sir Charles is very handsome."

Sally smiled at her. "He really is. Now away with you, you incorrigible girl."

"You want to talk to Amy about Lord Pascal," Meg said.

Amy blushed, although it was no secret in the

household that Pascal had set his sights on the widowed Lady Mowbray.

"I do indeed," Sally said. "Mind you go quietly upstairs. Morwenna's asleep."

"No, she's not. I saw the light in her window when we came in."

"Nonetheless, don't you go disturbing her."

"I won't." Meg made a pretty curtsy in Amy's direction. "Goodnight, Amy. Honestly I don't know how you resist Lord Pascal. I think he's gorgeous."

"That's enough out of you, miss," Sally said. "And you're not to dream of Amy's beau."

Amy laughed. "Oh, let her, if she wants to. I dreamed of him myself, when I was a giddy girl."

Meg's grin hinted that the young lady gracing the season's ballrooms hadn't completely overtaken the impudent hoyden of a few months ago. "So you're childhood sweethearts reunited?"

"Not at all. He didn't know I was alive, but I had a romantical streak when I was fourteen."

"Meg, it's time you were in bed, instead of asking rude questions," Sally said, although her attempts at sternness were never very convincing.

"Yes, Aunt." She paused at the door, and the humor left her eyes. "And thank you. I know I'm a trial to you, but I'm grateful for everything you're doing for me."

"Not that much of a trial." Sally's expression softened. "Away with you, mousekin."

Amy smiled after Meg as she left. "She's a lovely girl."

"She is. And I hope she finds happiness. I like Sir Charles, and he's been most particular in his attentions since he arrived in London last week."

"He has." Although in Amy's opinion, he was interested in Sally, rather than her pretty niece. She knew Sally well enough by now not to voice that opinion. Sally believed that at thirty, she was past the age of romance. "I like him, too."

"He's invited us to the Royal Academy tomorrow. I do hope Meg doesn't betray her complete ignorance of painting. Sir Charles is quite the connoisseur. Did you notice the Titian in his drawing room?"

Amy hid a smile. "I did indeed. Luckily you can talk pictures, if Meg finds herself at sea." Over supper, Sir Charles and Sally had enjoyed a lively discussion about Mr. Turner's latest works. Meg had been busy, telling Amy and Pascal about her father's stables. The chit mightn't know much about art, but she could wax eloquent on equine bloodlines.

Sally rose from her chair near the fire. "Would you like a brandy?"

A small glass of brandy was the perfect accompaniment to these late night chats. "Yes, please."

While Sally poured their drinks, a comfortable silence fell. It still astounded Amy how easily she and Sally had fallen into friendship. They were both lonely, and she'd learned to appreciate Sally's worldly experience and sound common sense.

Sally passed Amy a brandy and carried hers back to her chair. "I'm worried about Morwenna."

"I am, too." Amy sipped her drink. "But to give her her due, she's doing better than I thought she would."

"Oh, I agree. She puts on a great pretense of enjoying herself. But under the gaiety, she's still grieving."

Amy settled back and let the liquor and the fire melt away the night's tension. The strain of this prolonged torture of a courtship told on her. With every moment in Pascal's company, her control became more frayed. Tonight, he'd looked so disheartened, she'd nearly flung herself into his arms and begged him to kiss her.

But she was painfully aware that his lovers were always cheaply won, and just as easily forsaken. She couldn't bear to become another eager, forgettable woman in a long list of eager, forgettable women.

"Sally, she needed every ounce of courage she possessed to come to London and face the world again. She and Robert were deeply in love. Give her time. And don't forget that she's missing Kerenza." Kerenza was at Woodley with Silas and Caroline and all her Nash cousins. Morwenna knew her daughter was fine, but that didn't make the separation easier.

"I know she is. I just wish she was happy."

"Especially after you've tried so hard to give us a memorable few weeks."

Sally waved her glass in a dismissive gesture. "I've loved having you both to stay—and Meg, too."

"Your niece is a great success, and her popularity hasn't turned her head."

"No, she's a good child, if a little too inclined to mock the wisdom of her elders."

Amy sent Sally a disgusted look. "I wish you wouldn't do that."

"What?" Sally drained her brandy.

"Talk about yourself as if you've got one foot in the grave. You're beautiful, and you've got more energy than Morwenna and me combined. If you think society's gentlemen haven't noticed, you need spectacles."

Sally's lips twitched. "Shortsightedness is a sign of old age."

"And blind stubbornness is a sign of a closed mind."

Sally laughed, clearly discounting Amy's comments. "You're too kind. Why would anyone look at me when I'm with Meg, who's so young and vibrant?"

Amy shook her head. "Not every man wants an untried girl, Sally."

Sally's eyes sharpened. "Speaking of men who like women with some life experience, when are you going to put Pascal out of his misery?"

Amy's shoulders tautened, although she knew that this interrogation was inevitable. And also that Sally asked the question to shift the focus away from herself. "He's courting me."

"Which he's done assiduously for the last three

weeks. I've never seen the man work so hard to win a woman. Usually they're clamoring after him."

"That's part of the problem," Amy admitted, staring into her glass to avoid Sally's perceptive gaze. She'd never told her friends that Pascal wanted to marry her. Although since he'd become the perfect escort, he hadn't mentioned marriage. Quite possibly, he'd dismissed the idea, now Amy proved so much trouble.

"Oh, tosh. None of those women meant a farthing to him."

A chill ran down her spine. "You seem remarkably well informed," she said stiffly.

Dear God, had she been too naïve for words? Pascal and Sally were old friends and visibly comfortable together. Had they once been more than friends?

Scorn edged Sally's snort. "Tuck in your claws. We've never been lovers. I was faithful to my husband, and since his death, nobody has tempted me to err."

"Then why are you pushing me along the primrose path?" Amy said, ashamed of her petty jealousy.

Sally shrugged. "I'm not opposed to taking a lover. Perhaps I'll look around more seriously, once I've got Meg settled."

"You didn't answer my question."

"I don't know." A dreamy light that Amy had never seen before softened Sally's expression. "It's just that you and Pascal seem…right somehow. Like you fit. To be candid, I expected him to tumble you into bed that night you came in from the Bartletts' garden, looking like he'd kissed you into next week."

"Oh." Heat prickled Amy's cheeks. "You noticed."

"I could hardly miss it."

"You didn't say anything."

Sally smiled. "You were doing well without interference. But since then, you've turned as prim as a middle-aged governess, and he's tiptoeing around you as if terrified you'll shatter at the first touch."

"I want...I want him to prove he's genuinely interested."

Sally rolled her eyes. "He's so interested, he looks ready to cut his throat unless you show him a drop of kindness. Which would be a sad waste of a very pretty man."

Amy sent her friend a direct look. "By kindness, you mean let him seduce me."

Sally shrugged and refilled her glass. "Or you could seduce him. I hate to see you at odds, when it's perfectly obvious that you're both mad for one another."

"I've never...I've never taken a lover," Amy said unsteadily.

"Well, given dried-up old Wilfred Mowbray is the extent of your experience, it's time you did."

"Wilfred was a good man," she snapped, hearing the guilt lurking beneath her defense of her late husband. Because of course, Pascal excited her in ways that Wilfred never had.

"He was. But he's gone now. And he was always too old for a vivid creature like you." Sally set her glass on a side table. The understanding in her face made Amy feel that her friend guessed all her secrets. Including her aching longing to surrender to Pascal and sample this hot magic that put the whole world in a stew. "You need to see what a young, virile man can do for you."

"And that young, virile man is Lord Pascal?"

"He's certainly willing. I've never seen a man as…willing."

"It's a big step."

"And you're frightened."

Amy's lips twitched. "Terrified. And I can't quite believe he's attracted to me."

Compassion flooded Sally's face. "Oh, Amy, I hoped you'd got over this silly self-doubt. You're lovely and smart and unusual, and any man would be lucky to win you. I know it. Meg knows it. Morwenna knows it. All those men who line up to dance with you know it. Believe me, Lord Pascal knows it. The only person who doesn't know it is you."

"You make me sound so poor spirited," Amy said in a subdued voice. The brandy that had tasted so pleasant on her palate now burned like acid in her stomach.

Sally made a sweeping gesture. "No. Just inexperienced in the ways of the world. Pascal is eating his heart out for you."

"I'm not sure his heart is involved."

Sally's smile was arch. "Other parts of him certainly are. The man's turning into a complete wreck. I started out enjoying the sight of him topsy-turvy over a woman. After all, he's had enough ladies sighing over him. Now I can't help feeling sorry for him. If you want him, take him. If you don't, set the poor fellow loose."

It might reflect badly on her character, but Amy couldn't help relishing the thought of gorgeous Gervaise Dacre sick with desire for her humble self. She sucked in a breath and stiffened her backbone as she summoned all her courage. Perhaps it was time to dare.

Her voice emerged with unexpected steadiness. "I want him, all right."

Sally's smile was broad and approving. "In that case, do something about it."

CHAPTER TEN

*P*ascal mounted the shallow steps to Sally Norwood's door two at a time and brought down the knocker with a resounding crash. The butler opened the door and regarded him impassively. "Good morning, my lord."

"Lady Mowbray has asked to see me."

"Her ladyship is in the garden. Allow me to show you the way."

"Don't worry. I'll find her."

Ignoring the butler's disapproval, he strode past the man and through Sally's elegant house, until he reached the morning room with its doors open on the garden. April was the usual mixture of showers and sunshine—today was like the start of summer.

Or perhaps that was just how he felt this morning.

"I believe she's sitting beside the fountain, my lord." The butler had moved at a fair clip to keep pace.

"Thank you." He flashed the man a smile and ran outside and down the path. He'd been to parties here and headed unerringly for the secluded corner where a mossy stone cupid held a dolphin amid the play of waters.

"Pascal." Amy's joyous expression as she stood echoed the happiness exploding like fireworks in his heart. He strode up to her, boots crunching on the gravel, and caught her by the shoulders.

"Is it yes?"

Her eyes sparkled with indomitable spirit. "It's yes."

"My darling," he breathed, dragging her into his body for a kiss so hot it threatened to blast him to ash.

Too soon, she pulled free with a shaky laugh. "You gathered a lot from three words."

He kissed her again, quickly this time. He wanted to kiss her over and over again, until she was panting and trembling. Then he wanted to tumble her onto the grass, and toss her skirts up, and join her on a voyage to paradise.

But he maintained a shred of sense. And thank every angel in heaven, he'd have a chance to answer every fantasy. Soon.

The second sweetest word in the English language after "yes."

He cradled her head between his hands and studied her piquant face. At last the distance was gone. She looked flushed and delightfully ruffled. "When the three words are 'come to me,' I had an inkling what you meant. I've passed the test?"

The misty softness in her smile was new. His Amy was inclined to regard him with a skeptical eye. He applauded the change. It made him feel like a king.

"You have. I realized that I no longer doubted you. I was just frightened. That's no acceptable reason to avoid something."

He leaned forward and kissed her again. It was a mere three weeks since he'd kissed her, but it felt like three years. "So you're going to take me like a tonic for the good of your health?"

"Perhaps that's what you are."

His laugh was fond. That poignant tenderness was more powerful than ever. During the interminable delay, it had proven an awkward companion. "I promise by the time I'm finished with you, you'll feel much better."

"Wicked fellow." She linked her hands behind his neck.

"I am indeed. And I intend to devote that wickedness to your enjoyment. I'm hoping some wickedness might even rub off on you."

Her lips quirked. "That's already happened. I used to be perfectly respectable, devil take you."

She didn't sound like she minded too much. He couldn't help it. He kissed her again. She responded with sizzling enthusiasm, until he could manage only a single word. The question that thundered through every beat of his reckless heart. "When?"

She didn't pretend to misunderstand. "Not now. Meg and Sally will be home soon from their shopping, and Morwenna is inside writing letters."

"We could give her something interesting to write about."

"Too interesting. You need to stop kissing me."

"Never." To prove it, he kissed her again. This time he lingered over her lips, relishing how she welcomed him into the honeyed heat of her mouth. By the time he raised his head, they were both gasping for breath.

"When you kiss me, I can't think." Arousal clouded her eyes.

"I haven't been able to think since I met you." His voice descended into stark sincerity. "You make me so happy."

"You make me nervous and excited." She paused. "And happy. I'm sure I should regret this headlong dash into sin."

"Ah, sin," he said on a voluptuous sigh.

"You're incorrigible." She laughed and pushed him away.

He let her go, content now that he had her promise. "When, when, when?"

She caught his hand. "So impatient."

"Amy," he growled. "You've teased me enough."

She drew him down onto the charming stone bench where she'd sat watching the fountain. To his regret, she started to sound sensible again. How he'd loved seeing this clever, practical woman dizzy with excitement.

"It's not straightforward. We need to be careful. Any scandal will hurt Meg's chances. The world can't know she's sharing a house with Lord Pascal's mistress."

He liked the sound of that. He'd like the sound of Lord Pascal's wife even more, but today he was content to postpone that discussion. "I want you to myself all night."

Already she was shaking her head. "It's too risky."

He sighed. "When did you become adept at intrigue?"

Amy blushed and squeezed his hand. "I've...I've been thinking of this since our last kiss."

His laugh expressed astounded delight. "I had no idea. You've been so cold, I quite despaired of winning your favor."

"I'm sorry that I was such a coward."

"And you didn't trust me. But you do now. Your consent does me such honor."

Amy was back to looking misty-eyed. "I couldn't resist you."

She was a miracle, and he didn't deserve her. He sucked in a jagged breath to contain the vast wave of emotion that threatened to choke him. In silent homage, he raised her hand to his lips.

Pascal struggled to restore the lightness. She wasn't yet ready to hear what lay in his heart. He'd lured her to the threshold of a life together, but only careful handling would coax her across into a permanent place in his future. "So while you were busy tormenting me, you were hatching wanton plans?"

Her smile was tremulous. "I thought perhaps one afternoon…"

"*One* afternoon?"

She gave a nervous, excited spurt of laughter. "Let's not get ahead of ourselves. We usually go driving anyway. Perhaps instead of the park, we go to—"

"Heaven?"

Her breath caught, and her eyes darkened. "I hope so, although I'm so afraid I'll disappoint you. I'm sure… I'm sure you're used to more skillful lovers."

He couldn't bear to see her crippling doubt creeping back. Catching the back of her neck, he drew her up for another hungry kiss. "I want you, Amy. Only you."

"And I want you, Pascal."

He'd waited an eon to hear her say that. He trailed a finger down her cheek, then followed the sensitive nerve down the side of her neck. She shivered in response. There was so much sensuality locked up inside her. He ached to set it free.

Tomorrow…

"You know, given our licentious plans, you should call me Gervaise."

A soft smile curved her lips, and when his name emerged, it heated his blood like brandy. "Gervaise."

This time his kiss was gentle, and when he drew away, she clung to his shoulders. He suspected her head was swimming. His balance didn't feel too sturdy either. "Leave everything to me."

"I will. I'll see you tonight for dinner before the Lewis musicale."

"And will you grant me both waltzes from now on?"

The radiant emotion faded from her lovely face, but it was enough that he'd seen it. She mightn't be in love with him, but she hovered close. He'd wager his life on it. And Amy Mowbray's love was a gift he didn't take lightly.

"I'd like to give you every dance. But it's not discreet."

He bit back the retort that if she agreed to marry him, discretion could go to Hades. He'd brought her this far. Surely after sharing her body, she'd take that last step. "I can live with that. Hell, now you've said yes, I can live with anything."

She leaned forward, and this time, she kissed him. Her boldness blasted heat through his veins. The time between now and consummation stretched wider than the Atlantic.

But by God, he had now.

He wrapped his arms around her and draped her across his lap. The brush of her hip across his swollen cock set stars exploding behind his eyes.

For one moment, she lay softly against him, then

she drew back to regard him with heavy eyes. "Gervaise…"

He loved to hear his name on her lips. "Don't look at me like that, or I won't go."

"If you stay, we'll end up shocking Sally's gardeners."

He gave a huff of amusement and stole another kiss before he let her sit up. "I have arrangements to make."

"And we'll meet tonight."

"If you look at me like that, everyone will know what's in store."

"I can't help it. I feel like I'm about to take flight."

Pascal kissed her hand again, not trusting himself to kiss her lips and retain the will to leave. And he intended to make everything perfect for her. That meant putting some thought into his plans and giving orders to his staff. "Tomorrow we'll take to the sky. Will you walk me to the back gate? In this state, I don't want to run into Sally or Meg."

Amy glanced down at him and blushed. "What about your carriage?"

"The moment I got your note, I dashed over."

"Not even time to harness your horses?"

"Not one second. And it's only a ten-minute walk. That I did in five."

He'd been hard put not to run, but while she was his mistress, not his wife, he intended to shield her name. She was the next Lady Pascal, even if she hadn't yet admitted it. On their wedding day, he wanted her to hold her head high.

Pray God, that wasn't far away.

"Oh, Gervaise..." she sighed and tumbled into his arms again.

It was considerably later when she let him out the back gate with a kiss and a whispered promise of tomorrow.

CHAPTER ELEVEN

*a*s Gervaise's carriage rolled up to the pretty little manor house outside Windsor, Amy's stomach churned with terror and anticipation.

"Second thoughts?" Gervaise asked gently.

She'd spent most of the drive from London silent and pressed close to his side. The warmth of his big male body had helped to counter her rioting nerves. It was another lovely day, and once they'd left London, rampant spring had surrounded them all the way.

"An army of them," she admitted, firming her grip on his brawny arm.

"You can still change your mind."

She cast him a doubtful glance, but that remarkable face under the curling brim of his stylish hat was serious. "That's very sporting of you."

"You look like you're about to face the Spanish Inquisition."

Her brief laugh was bleak. "That bad?"

He smiled with that hint of tenderness that always caught her on the quick and made her foolish heart cramp with longing. "Worse."

"Kiss me."

Those dark gold brows arched in inquiry. "Before I take you back to London?"

"Before I step out of this carriage, and you show me what all those wild women have taught you."

His lips curved in appreciation—and a relief that soothed her fears. It proved he didn't take her for granted. "We'll need more than one afternoon for that."

Before she could respond to his intriguing remark, he leaned in and kissed her, pressing her back against the brass rail behind the carriage seat.

She expected passion, but there was just more of that piercing tenderness. The sweetness seemed almost innocent. Absurd when she was about to give her body to a man who wasn't her husband.

"Will you stay?" he murmured, breath warm on her face.

"Yes."

"Thank you." He stared into her eyes, as if seeking out any lingering doubts. She knew he'd find them, but she was also sure he'd see her yearning.

Inevitably yearning overpowered her apprehension. Or she wouldn't be here at all.

A faint smile kicked up the corners of his beautiful

mouth, and he glanced toward the house. "What do you think?"

He'd kept their destination secret, although last night at the musicale, she'd tried to pry details out of him. The famous Italian diva had wasted her artistry on Amy, who had spent the evening in a daze. The only time she'd come alive to the moment was when she'd spoken to Gervaise. Even then she'd been jumpy and preoccupied, convinced every person in that worldly crowd must know of her imminent fall from grace.

This morning, Gervaise's note had arrived on her breakfast tray. He invited her to luncheon in the country and asked her to be ready at eleven. Because she'd lain awake most of the night and only fallen asleep near dawn, she had to rush to dress.

She'd left the house without encountering her friends, thank goodness. Morwenna was walking in the park—Amy wasn't nearly ready to confide her improper plans to her sister-in-law. Meg and Sally weren't up yet, although Sally would guess the truth when she read Amy's note about visiting the country with Lord Pascal.

Amy didn't mind Sally knowing. She just didn't want to talk about it.

When the curricle turned down a tree-lined drive, she hadn't been sure what to expect. What she found was a pocket manor, like a full-size dolls house.

Now she studied the perfectly proportioned façade and smiled. "It's lovely. How did you find it?"

"It's mine. The tenants left a month ago, and the new people don't move in until June." He clicked his tongue to the horses and steered them around the building to a neat stable block. "If we go to an inn, someone could see us. And at my townhouse, the servants might let slip that I entertained a lady."

She began to relax, although her heart still banged against her ribs like a trapped bird trying to escape its cage. "You've thought about this."

"I don't take this privilege lightly." They rolled into the shadowy, hay-scented interior with its rows of empty stalls. "I'll never do anything to cause you harm."

She looked around, puzzled, when no eager groom rushed to take the horses. "It's like an enchanted castle in a fairytale. Where is everyone? Asleep for a hundred years because a princess pricked her finger on a spindle?"

He smiled. "I've given the staff the afternoon off."

More thoughtfulness. Everything Gervaise did today betrayed meticulous care and consideration. She'd never felt so cherished. Sternly she reminded herself that she had no intention of losing her head over Gervaise Dacre.

But she feared it was already too late.

As they crunched across the gravel forecourt to the graceful set of steps leading up to the imposing door,

Amy held hands with Gervaise. They climbed the wide stone stairs, and he released her to fish in his pocket for a large iron key that also seemed to come from a fairytale.

She stepped into an airy hall, with high windows and chessboard tiles on the floor. Vases of massed spring flowers perfumed the air. He'd turned the house into a bower of earthly delights.

"Oh, Gervaise, I'm speechless." She paused a few paces inside the room to draw a deep breath. "And all for me?"

"All for you." He closed the door after him, but remained beside it. Without shifting his gaze from her, he took off his hat and gloves and set them on a chair.

She removed her gloves and bonnet, placing them on a chest under the window. "You've been busy since yesterday."

Gervaise made her feel so special. How on earth had she managed to hold out against him for over three weeks?

"I want you to smile when you look back on today." He removed his voluminous driving coat, then came forward and helped her with the tight pelisse. "There's champagne and a cold collation in the dining room. Are you hungry? I promised that I'd feed you when I invited you here."

Emotion jammed her throat and roughened her laugh. "I can't tell you how much I appreciate the trouble you've taken."

He leaned one elegant hip against the chest and watched her steadily. She shivered with anticipation and pleasure. The desire in his eyes made her feel free and powerful and, for the first time in her life, truly beautiful.

"Try."

She swept a dazzled gaze over the flower-filled room. "I was afraid I'd feel shabby. But standing here with you, it's like we share a glorious secret."

He smiled. "I'm glad."

Amy realized she felt more than beautiful. She felt brave. She'd hesitated enough. It was time to take a chance on what her heart had wanted since her first glimpse of him, so many years ago.

Stepping toward the oak staircase that curved up to what she guessed were the bedrooms, she held out her hand. "I don't want to wait anymore." Her voice was still husky. "I've waited too long already. Take me upstairs."

Joy transfigured his face. She realized that despite her spoken consent, and the kisses they'd shared, and her presence here now, he hadn't been entirely sure of her.

In a few eager strides, he crossed the room and caught her up for another of those world-shaking kisses. She should be accustomed to them by now—but every time he kissed her, the earth set off on a drunken jig through the stars.

In one powerful movement, he swept her up into

his arms and began to mount the stairs. Amy gasped and flung one arm around his powerful neck. "Gervaise, I can walk."

His low laugh made her stomach clench with longing. "Why walk when you can fly?"

"You're showing off," she said, to hide how this madly romantic gesture made her pulse race.

"Of course I am. I'm seeking a certain lady's approval."

She laid her head on his shoulder as he rounded the first landing, seemingly unwinded. His elegance was misleading. The arms that held her with such ease were hard with muscle. And he was so delightfully warm. This was like curling up beside a roaring fire on a cold winter's day.

"She already approves," she murmured, placing her hand over the place where his heart thudded hard and steady. Perhaps she hadn't been far wrong when she'd wondered if this house belonged in a fairytale. Right now she felt more like a magical princess than a mere mortal woman.

"My campaign must be working."

"Don't rest on your laurels," she said drily, as he carried her along a hallway. But it was impossible to cling to her level-headed self, when a handsome prince carried her away to ravish her.

They swung through an open door to a beautiful bedroom, done out in the style of last century. Windows opened onto the bright afternoon, and the air smelled of beeswax, and the fresh flowers ranged on every flat surface.

"Goodness," Amy said faintly, her heart taking another dizzy swoop. "There mustn't be a flower left in London."

"Do you like it?" He stopped in the middle of the room and stared down at her.

She read the genuine question in those deep blue eyes. "I love it." She stretched up to place a clumsy kiss on his lips. "Thank you."

He angled his head to anchor the kiss. "Any time."

Heat sizzled through her, promised more heat to come. Impatience set her blood rushing. The excruciating wait was over, and it was time to give in to her craving for this beautiful man.

The hands she linked behind his neck were steady, although she'd expected to suffer a storm of nerves when she yielded to him. "Take me to bed, Gervaise."

"With pleasure."

A few steps, and he flung back the covers to reveal crisp white sheets. Gently he set her down. The clean sharpness of lavender teased her senses.

"I love this house." She pushed up against the heaped pillows. "How can you bear to rent it out?"

The fleeting silence held a strangely discordant edge. But she forgot that odd, bristling instant when she watched him tug off his dark blue coat and lay it across a brocade chair near the unlit fire. Excitement coiled in her belly and made her skin prickle with expectation. Soon, soon they'd be naked together, and she'd at last discover sensuality's mysteries.

"I rarely use it. It's very old-fashioned."

"In a charming way."

His eyes lit as he surveyed her, lying before him in her pink silk dress. "Speaking of charming, you look delectable."

"Thank you." She sent him a sheepish smile. "I know it was terribly romantic when you put me on the bed, but undressing will be easier if I stand up."

He laughed softly and crossed to offer her his hand. "Let me help."

"Thank you." She accepted his hand and rose from the bed. In the last weeks, she must have touched his hand a thousand times. Now, the contact resonated like music with all that was to come. "I'll help you, too."

She reached up to untie his neck cloth, letting it drift to the floor. His shirt fell open, revealing a hard masculine chest beneath. Unable to resist, she placed her hand flat on that golden skin and felt him shudder in reaction. He was so warm. She raked her fingers through the curls of golden hair across his pectorals.

Even now he undressed, her courage didn't desert her. She'd expected to feel shy and awkward and inadequate. But this unpretentious house and the efforts Gervaise had taken to please her banished her misgivings.

When Sally had suggested that she should seduce Lord Pascal, it had seemed a bizarre idea. But here in this quiet room on this sunny afternoon, it didn't seem so outlandish.

This close, she caught his delicious scent. Clean male with a hint of healthy sweat. Lemon soap. Horses. Leather. Wilfred had smelled like an old man—an old, sick man toward the end. Gervaise smelled like a vital male in his prime.

Amy surrendered to wanton impulse and leaned into him, breathing deeply. She pressed her lips to his chest, tasting the salt on his skin. The tickle of his hair against her face reminded her that this was no fairytale, but a deeply carnal encounter.

Suddenly it felt like they had all the time in the world. He held her hips, but seemed content to let her continue to take the lead, despite her inexperience. Languorously, she stroked his chest, then unbuttoned his blue silk waistcoat. Her fingers remained steady and sure as they slid the waistcoat off his shoulders.

Gervaise reached for her, but she stepped out of reach. "Let me do this."

"You're driving me mad," he groaned. Standing before her in his loose white shirt and fawn breeches, he looked disheveled and gorgeous.

"Good. I want you so much."

His smile was wry. "Not as much as I want you."

When she glanced up at his face, stern and beautiful as a Donatello carving, she almost believed him. "I've been plotting to get you to myself since I was fourteen."

"If only I'd known."

She didn't waste time on regrets. They'd met again at the right time. He wrenched his shirt over his head and hurled it into the corner.

The superb view made the breath snag in her throat. "Dear God, you're magnificent."

"Amy…" he began, but when she raised her hands to release her hair, whatever he meant to say was lost as he watched her draw the pins free. At the sight of her hair tumbling about her shoulders, his eyes flared with hunger.

She stepped forward and twined her arms around his neck. She could hardly bear to go even an instant without touching him. "Kiss me."

Luscious, dark, succulent cooperation left her head swimming and her knees weak. Slowly he lifted away, as she struggled to remain upright on legs that threatened to fold beneath her.

"My turn?" he murmured.

Reluctantly she opened her eyes. His taste lingered on her lips. "Not yet."

He bit back another groan and buried his hands in her hair. "Have pity."

"Oh, no." Amy ran her hands over his skin again. It was such a luxury, touching him like this. The firm chest, the wide shoulders, the powerful back. At his sides, his fists opened and closed, and by the time she scored her nails across his nipples, he was shaking.

Who would have thought she could make this sophisticated man shake?

Power surged higher. Daringly she released the buttons on his breeches. The intriguing bulge inside them beckoned. With trembling hands, she revealed his hardness.

At first sight of him, a gasp escaped her. Gervaise's virility awed her, and the nerves that she hoped she'd conquered jumped up to snatch away her confidence.

She'd reached to touch him, but galloping uncertainty made her pause. Before she could withdraw, he caught her hand and pressed it against him. Every drop of moisture evaporated from her mouth, as she held his heat and power.

"Like this," he murmured, shaping her hand around him. He jerked under her tentative caress, and she instinctively tightened her grip. A low growl of masculine pleasure was her reward.

It turned out her confidence hadn't fled after all. His response did wonders for her self-assurance. With voluptuous pleasure in what she did, Amy began to stroke him.

As he grew larger under her brazen caress, she watched his face. His eyes were half-closed, and a hectic flush marked those slashing cheekbones. A frown drew his eyebrows together, as if what she did tested the outer reaches of his limits.

When she squeezed, he opened his eyes fully. The dilated pupils took over most of the blue and betrayed his excitement. "Let me touch you," he grated out, his usually melodious baritone as rough as gravel.

"Yes," she whispered, swaying forward. She'd reached a point where she didn't want to tease anymore. She just wanted Gervaise. "Touch me."

"Amy..." he groaned and caught her hand, crushing it against him for one last breathtaking moment. He hauled her into a kiss so urgent, it left her gasping.

CHAPTER TWELVE

*R*emaining still under Amy's touch pushed Pascal until he teetered on the edge. What a glorious surprise she turned out to be. He'd expected to need to coax her into revealing her sensuality. Long ago, he'd realized that for a widow, she was close to innocent.

So when she'd tugged off his neck cloth and kissed his bare chest, his heart slammed to an astounded stop. Then he'd stood trembling as with unashamed enjoyment, she touched him. Finally she'd laid her hand on his cock, and the pleasure threatened to immolate him.

All impulse to prolong the preliminaries into the evening vanished. He'd never wanted a woman as much as he wanted Amy Mowbray. Now, praise God, he was going to have her.

He drew out of that blazing kiss and stepped away to sit on the bed. Clumsy with urgency, he yanked off his boots and flung them aside. Then he stood and directed his attention to unwrapping this incomparable gift fate had given him. Quickly he unlaced the pretty rose-pink dress and let it fall to the floor. Her filmy undergarments soon followed.

When at last she was naked, he released the breath he felt he'd held all day. She'd led him such a chase, he'd never been sure of her. Even when he'd carried her upstairs. But her melting expression now told him she cast aside reluctance and offered him everything.

The compulsion to rush to the end while she was here and she was his set his blood alight, but he made himself linger to admire her. "You're temptation personified."

Her body was lithe and graceful, more athletic than he'd imagined in those feverish nights when he'd lain awake wanting her. Full, high breasts. Rich, female curves. Long legs.

Nervously Amy raised one hand to cover the brown curls below her pale stomach. The other hand hovered above her beaded pink nipples.

"I've...I've never been naked with a man before," she admitted in a cracked voice. "Wilfred came to me in darkness, and we always kept our clothes on."

How much she had to discover. How much he had to show her. "There's no need to be shy. You're glorious."

Despite her pink cheeks, she tilted her chin and subjected his body to a thorough inspection. Heat sizzled through him, and his balls tightened in anticipation.

"I want to please you."

"You do." He ran his hand down her arm, delighting in her silky skin, and laced his fingers with hers. "You will."

Her fingers twined around his with a swift trust that made his heart somersault. Pascal leaned in and placed his lips on hers, leashing his ravenous passion.

She responded with the sweetness so essential to her nature. Under his gentle exploration, she sighed, and the tension gradually seeped from her body. Taking exquisite care, he began to touch her, finding the places that made her tremble. His hands learned the line of her back, the dip of her waist, the flare of her hips, the lushness of her buttocks. Deliberately he avoided her breasts and sex. His control balanced on a knife edge.

He nudged her toward the bed and broke her fall when she tumbled back onto the sheets. She was panting with excitement.

He pulled away to strip off his breeches, until he, too, was naked. When she stared at him with what looked like wonder, he blushed for the first time in twenty years.

"I'm a lucky girl."

He gave a broken laugh. "Not as lucky as I am."

"We'll argue about that later."

"Much later." He had difficulty summoning

coherent speech. The endless beat of desire was too powerful. He came down over her, sliding his hips between her spread thighs. The friction of skin on skin was delicious.

"Yes." Readily she curved her hands over his shoulders and raised her knees, cradling him closer to where he longed to be. Her musky arousal mingled with the scent of the flowers. For the rest of his life, he'd think of this as the perfume of paradise.

When he bent to take her nipple between his lips, she jerked and cried out, digging her fingers into his back. He reached down to stroke her cleft, dipping his fingers into the hot female honey.

When she was writhing in demand against the sheets, he lifted his head to see her face. Her eyes were half shut, and a flush colored her cheeks.

"Don't stop," she murmured, sliding one hand up to caress his jaw. "I love what you're doing."

Ruthlessness tinged this kiss, then he took her other nipple into his mouth, flicking his tongue over it again and again until she quivered and moaned. Between her legs, his hand moved more purposefully. His thumb brushed the center of her pleasure, and she released a sharp little cry.

Carefully he slid a finger into her. She tightened in swift welcome, and he gritted his teeth against spiraling arousal. How he longed to taste her there. To bring her to climax with his tongue. But his primitive, irresistible need to claim her made further delay unthinkable.

He caught her thighs and held them apart. On a powerful surge, he rose and thrust forward. As he pushed into her body, she hissed with satisfaction and dug her nails into his back. The sharp sting heightened the avalanche of sensations overwhelming him.

Tight, hot and wet, she clenched around him. How could a man survive such bliss?

She arched up and kissed his neck. "Gervaise."

Just his name. No more. But it was enough. He heard every ounce of her pleasure in the single word.

With heavy strokes, Pascal moved, staking his possession with every plunge. The soft music of her moans, the grip of her body, the flutter of her hands against the bare skin of his back and arms, all fed his fierce arousal. His thrusts intensified, pushing her into the mattress. Still she rose to meet him, lifting her hips to take him deeper.

Her breath escaped in erratic gusts. Pascal was so close, but through his approaching crisis, he held back. He needed her to go first, to find what she'd never known before. She jerked her hips higher, but still didn't cross over into release.

He shifted to lean on one elbow so he could touch her and take her over. For a fraught moment, she tautened into quaking stillness. He rose on his arms to slide into her again, and she cried out in astonished discovery. The storm finally broke and made her shake and sob under the onslaught of pleasure. The eyes that met his shone liquid gold.

Through her shuddering peak, he poised over her, battling to hold still. The moment stretched into rapturous agony.

At last, with a guttural growl, he wrenched free to spill his seed on the soft curve of her stomach.

In blind, primal release, he pumped his passion onto her skin. Then he slumped beside her, burying his face in the pillows.

Pascal felt elated, exhausted, free. While some wicked, hungry part of him regretted that he hadn't flooded her womb with sweet heat.

Amy lay naked and shaking beside Gervaise, as those unearthly, shattering feelings slowly ebbed. The peak had flung her clear of the world and sent her soaring through blazing light. She still felt lost among the stars. She'd had no idea. No idea at all.

Now the world was made anew. And her principal reaction was poignant gratitude. That fate had seen fit to place her in Lord Pascal's path. That she'd finally mustered the courage to act on the attraction. That she'd had a chance to discover the magic a man and a woman could conjure from two naked bodies in a bed.

She spared a moment's pity for Wilfred, who had never known this ecstasy. The few times he'd come to her, their union had been quick, fumbling. Hidden, because he felt ashamed of wanting her, even though she was his wife.

There had been none of the unabashed enjoyment Gervaise had taken in her. And Wilfred's discomfort with his physical needs had made her feel awkward and ugly, so she'd never asked more from him.

Now she looked back on her marriage and thought how sad it was that delight had been a stranger. Wilfred had been a good man. She was sorry this rich fulfillment had been denied to him.

The irony was that she'd felt a thousand times more shame, lying with her lawful husband, than with her dissolute lover. She was now a fallen woman, and she'd never known such happiness.

Clearly she was a brazen hussy.

"Why are you smiling?" Gervaise asked softly.

She turned to find him resting his head on his arm and studying her. "I think you know."

When attractive amusement crinkled his eyes, his physical beauty struck her anew. She'd never seen his expression so unguarded. With a shock, she realized that even with her, he'd maintained a slight detachment.

Long ago, she'd guessed that Gervaise's outstanding looks were as much burden as blessing. But she only now understood how he cultivated a constant emotional distance. Essential, she supposed, when the whole world wanted something from you.

"I can guess." His kiss expressed a searching tenderness that made her toes curl against the rumpled
sheets. "Or at least hope."

The thread of intimacy spinning between them was
too fragile to bear the weight of vows and plans. She
drew him down for another kiss, trying to tell him
without words how he'd changed her. Because after
this afternoon, she'd never go back to being frightened,
crippled Amy Mowbray, closing herself away from life
and joy and danger.

He rolled out of bed and crossed to the washstand.
How she admired his comfortable nakedness. Even
now, after those extraordinary moments in his arms,
she wasn't quite so brave.

Amy was reaching for the sheet when he splashed
some water from the ewer into a bowl and began to
wash. Her hand stilled, and she lay transfixed. Something about observing this private activity strengthened the invisible net drawing them together.

Once he'd finished, he poured fresh water into the
bowl and approached the bed. "Let me wash you."

His seed was sticky on her stomach. She thought
back to the fiery moments when she'd burst through
into transcendent pleasure, followed by the faint disappointment, even then, when he'd withdrawn.

As a man of honor should, he'd protected her. But
the abrupt intrusion of worldly practicality into that
profound experience had tainted her wholehearted
surrender.

A baby out of wedlock would be a disaster. During her marriage, she'd never conceived, but Wilfred had been old and mostly indifferent. She had a suspicion Gervaise's seed was considerably more potent.

This chagrin was lunacy for a woman who wasn't sure she wanted to marry again. Although if she were to choose a husband, she began to think Gervaise mightn't be a bad option.

"Thank you," she murmured, as he ran the cloth over her skin. She lay unmoving under his care, still not completely at ease with her nakedness. "For everything."

"I don't want you regretting anything we do," he said softly, rinsing the flannel in the lukewarm water, then returning to his task. He parted her legs, and the water felt marvelous on the hot, swollen flesh between her thighs.

It was years since she'd had a man in her bed—and Gervaise's proportions were considerably more generous than Wilfred's. And he'd been much more energetic. She'd loved what he'd done, but now she felt stretched and a little sore.

"I should feel more remorseful than I do," she admitted. "And shocked."

"Yet you don't?" He dropped the cloth into the water with a small splash and returned the bowl to the washstand.

"I must be irredeemable." Amy pushed higher on the pillows and shoved the heavy fall of hair back from her

face. She didn't want anything to obscure the spectacular view. Female appreciation warmed her blood as
her gaze traced his strong back and legs, and the firm
globes of his buttocks.

When he turned to face her, the interest in his eyes
echoed the interest his body betrayed. Late sunlight
poured through the window and traced him in gold, as
if even the sun couldn't resist contributing to his splendor. "Oh, I hope so."

She laughed. "You're no use."

His eyes narrowed with purpose. "I dare you to say
that in ten minutes."

"Ten minutes?"

"Maybe five." His smile deepened. "Tell me what
you feel."

She stretched against the bedhead, luxuriating in
how his eyes focused on her breasts. Her bashfulness
receded under his blatant admiration. Nakedness had
its advantages. "Naughty certainly."

"That's a start."

Her voice lowered to seriousness. "I never imagined
I could feel like I did in your arms. You have a gift, my
lord."

Unexpectedly, her heartfelt praise displeased him.
"It's not just me. It's the two of us together. You're
incomparable, Amy. And the only person who doesn't
recognize that is you."

She didn't want to ponder her shortcomings. After
all, the afternoon would soon be over, and she'd have to

go back to London and pretend she was the same prag-matic creature she'd been before today. She stretched out her hand. "I'll tell you something—I feel like the most beautiful woman in the world when you touch me."

His smile filled with the sweetness that always turned her mind to soup. "Then it must be time to touch you again."

"An excellent suggestion," she said, fearing that she smirked. Difficult to resist smugness when he looked at her like that. Like she was a piece of Turkish delight, and he wanted to snap her up with one bite of his straight, white teeth.

Gervaise took her hand, but didn't yet push her down for another passionate wrestle. "Are you sure you're ready to do this? I'm not a brute. I can wait until next time."

Her eyebrows arched in taunting inquiry. "Next time?"

"I don't want a passing conquest." He lifted her hand, and the graze of his lips across her skin made her quake with anticipation. Stronger than before, now she knew just what she anticipated. "If I had my way, I'd whisk you away to some secret haven and sate every appetite. Day after glorious day."

For a dazed interval, she stared into those intense, perfect features and imagined what that would be like. Hour after hour in Gervaise's bed. Night after night. Taking their pleasure, until they collapsed with exhaustion in a tangle of naked limbs. Then seeking pleasure anew. Nobody nearby to interrupt or observe or judge.

And endless time to talk to him. She wanted him. Of course she did. But more than that, she longed to see into his soul. He was such a compelling mixture of rake and hero.

A bird called from a tree outside and shattered the alluring fantasy of escape. It was impossible. She wasn't some starry-eyed milkmaid in thrall to the amorous plowboy. With fishing rod or not.

She had responsibilities, obligations. If she forsook her reputation, she'd damage her family's future. Silas and Helena and Robert all had children who would suffer from gossip about a notorious aunt.

Amy beat back the sudden wistfulness. Regret held no sway in this room. What she had was the fulfillment of a dream. Asking for more was greedy.

She rose to lace her arms around Gervaise's powerful neck and draw him down for a bold, open-mouthed kiss. When at last he raised his head, she smiled and told herself to be content with the present.

"We're somewhere secret now," she murmured. "Let's take advantage of it while we can."

CHAPTER THIRTEEN

*C*arefully Pascal closed the library door, shutting out the sounds of the crowded ballroom from the other side of the house. The music and chatter from Lady Frame's party turned into a distant hum.

Now all he heard was the insistent pump of his blood and the siren call of temptation.

Amy faced him, standing before the large mahogany desk under the curtained windows. She wore crimson, as if their passion found its inevitable color. The melting surrender in her expression sent a jolt of arousal through him.

He leaned his back against the door and turned the key in the lock without looking. He was too busy drinking in every detail of this woman he wanted more with every day.

A slow, sensual smile curved her lips. The smile was

new and spoke of a woman incandescent with sensual power. Such a change from the lovely, but wary lady he'd first met. Now her beauty blazed like a beacon. Need, bright and burning as lightning, sizzled along his veins.

The luxuriant pile of tawny hair held a tantalizing hint of untidiness, a reminder of how it cascaded free when he hauled her into bed. Her hazel eyes were more gold than green, glittering with brazen interest. Her creamy breasts mounded above the daringly low bodice and rose and fell with her uneven breathing.

"You're here." His voice rang with satisfaction.

"Of course I am," she said with unconcealed excitement. "It's been three days since we were alone."

He loved that she didn't try to hide her need. "We've been driving every afternoon."

Her grimace was charming. "You know what I mean."

He did indeed. And he'd suffered, as apparently had she. It was a fortnight since those extraordinary hours at the house near Windsor. They'd managed two more meetings there. Both brimming with unforgettable pleasure. Both cruelly short.

For the first time in Pascal's life, a few snatched moments with a lover weren't enough. He was tired of sneaking around. He wanted the world to acknowledge Amy Mowbray as his. He wanted a wife.

How the mighty had fallen.

"You're wearing my bracelet."

She raised her slender wrist until the stones caught the uncertain light. "I am."

The memory of the occasion a week ago when she'd accepted the diamonds shuddered through him. She'd sprawled naked across the rumpled sheets at his manor, and the sinking sun had painted her pink and gold.

"And is that a new dress?"

"It is."

"I approve."

All night, he'd been unable to look away from the tall woman in red. A woman who danced with every blockhead in the room except Pascal, damn it. He'd reserved his two dances. The supper one—which they now missed—and the final waltz. Every day, the restrictions placed around pursuing a respectable mistress chafed more painfully.

Devil take it, if she married him, he could dance with her all night and let gossip go hang. Hell, they could stay home and forget dancing altogether.

"I'm glad." Their commonplace words floated on a turbulent sea of unspoken yearning.

The room was dimly lit—Lady Frame didn't want her guests skulking in the library when they should be adorning her glittering ballroom. The light fell across Amy from behind and turned her fascinating, change-able eyes to mystery.

"I look forward to stripping it off you."

With a poignant echo of her old uncertainty, her

hand fluttered above her sumptuous bosom. "In the middle of a ball, that might take things a little far."

"I can dream."

She reached for him. "I've been dreaming of you."

She'd never been a coy woman. From the first, he'd recognized her rare authenticity in the world of appearances and illusion he inhabited. In some profound way, she turned him into a good man. If she ever took that feeling away, she'd leave him desolate.

Such magic she had. And he'd fallen under her spell before he learned to fear her ability to wreak devastation upon him.

"Good dreams?" Pascal straightened away from the door and approached her. Every time he saw her, he paused to thank whatever forces blessed him with this extraordinary woman.

To his delight, she flushed and avoided his eyes. "I doubt if my vicar would describe them that way."

"How intriguing." He caught her hand and, with sudden determination, tugged her into his arms. "Tell me more."

"Perhaps later," she gasped, as her soft breasts met his cream brocade waistcoat. Her heat seeped through his clothing and stoked his desire. She was warm in body and soul. Until he met her, he'd lived in an arctic wasteland. "You're far too used to getting your own way, my lord."

"My lord?"

She tilted her face up, and he caught the spark of

mischief in her eyes. A few weeks ago, her fire had been banked. Now it flamed high for all to see. "Gervaise."

She wouldn't know this, but whenever she spoke his name, her expression softened in a way that turned his cynical heart to pudding. "That's better."

"It would be even better if you kissed me."

"I'm savoring the moment." He strung out the tantalizing delay.

Her fingers curved against his neck in a caress of such tenderness that she stole his breath. Never before had he known this heady combination of passion and affection and respect with a lover. It was as addictive as opium and twice as sweet.

"Savor the moment a little more quickly," she said drily. "Mr. Harslett has requested the quadrille after supper."

"Damn it, don't I know it? Why the devil do you let those other blackguards paw you?"

She smiled and rose on her toes to trace his jaw with her lips. Heat seared a path across his skin, and he started shaking. She was the only woman in Creation who could make him tremble. The whisper of her breath across his face spurred his pulse to a gallop. "You want to be the only blackguard who paws me?"

"Hell, yes," he hissed and turned his head to catch her mouth with his.

Immediately she curved against him, and her lips opened with a hunger that matched his. He lashed his arms around her, bringing her so close that she could be in no doubt of his readiness. She tasted of spicy honey with a hint of champagne. Her female scent filled his senses, made him drunk on her fragrance.

"Damn it, Amy, this is excruciating." Reluctantly he drew away. "Will you meet me tomorrow?"

She raised a gloved hand to stroke his cheek. "Silas and Caro are down from Leicestershire, and we're spending the day together."

"Come to me instead. Please." In his rakish past, he'd never pleaded with a woman.

"I can't." Her smile conveyed regret, but damn it, not enough. "You know I can't."

He scowled, knowing he was unfair, but incapable of hiding his frustration. "All I know is that I feel like I'm starving to death for want of you."

She cast a sideways glance toward the couch near the fire. He read the thought before she spoke, and a shocked thrill shuddered through him. She was the most exciting woman he'd ever known. Through the heady progress of their affair, she'd become breathtakingly reckless.

"We could do something tonight." Her voice was a thread of sound, and pink tinged her cheeks. "Here."

Eagerness vied with caution. He'd never regarded himself as the chivalrous type, but he guarded Amy's good name like a sheepdog guarded a lamb. "That's not why I asked you to meet me."

"I know." Her voice strengthened, and she spoke

with more urgency. He couldn't doubt that she wanted this. "But with the crowds at supper, nobody will notice our absence. Even if they do, they'll think we're in the gardens, or admiring the art in the gallery. There's time."

His cock responded predictably to her suggestion. "It's still risky."

She pressed her lips to his in a quick kiss that promised more to come. "You're not the only one who hungers, Gervaise."

Heat rippled through him. Heat—and gratitude for lovely women who turned a man's world to bright sunshine. How could he resist? He caught her hand, then stared thwarted at the row of tiny buttons fastening her long red gloves.

Wanton anticipation vibrated in her laugh. "It will take you an hour to undo them. And another hour to do them up again. My maid nearly went cross-eyed, dressing me tonight."

"Blasted impractical rags you women wear," he muttered.

A soft huff of amusement. "I thought you liked my new ensemble."

"I want your hands on me."

"I do, too." She curled her gloved fingers around his and drew him toward the couch. "Next time."

He resisted. "I have a better idea."

An idea that threatened to incinerate his brain to ash, it was so audacious.

So far in bed, they hadn't progressed much beyond the basics. The pleasure of having her lying beneath him was more than enough. He never tired of the rapturous surprise glowing in her eyes with every climax. It still appalled him that her old duffer of a husband hadn't had the gumption to value what he had. Wilfred Mowbray had had paradise in his grasp, and he hadn't known it.

But perhaps tonight offered Pascal a chance to try something a little more exotic.

Curiosity lit her eyes to bright green. "Oh?"

He caught her hips and turned her toward the desk, then released her to take off his coat. "Trust me."

"I trust you." Her ready agreement made him smile. It had taken him a long time to gain her trust. Now he had it, he intended to keep it. "Do you want me to get onto the desk?"

"You don't sound shocked."

She shrugged, although intriguingly her blush intensified. "I bow to your greater experience."

He wanted to tell her that what they shared beggared his experience. With Amy, there was an emotional link he'd never felt before. Old, familiar moves seemed new and meaningful. But right now, she was ready and willing, and time ran away with a speed he cursed to Hades.

Soon he'd have to settle their future, persuade her to marry him, perhaps even confess what lay in his heart. But not now. Now pleasure and a beautiful, ardent woman awaited.

He shifted behind her and rubbed luxuriously against her buttocks, holding her upper arms in a caressing grip. "I commend your bold spirit, my love."

She swayed back, and he turned his face into the soft mass of her hair. She never reacted to his endearments. But then, why should she? He'd called so many women his darling and his sweetheart, and meant nothing special.

Sometimes, God forgive him, an endearment hid that he'd forgotten a lover's name. With Amy, though, he meant every tender word—and he paid the price for his thoughtlessness, because the one woman who should believe him didn't notice.

"You've made me brave," she murmured. "Let me go, so I can get onto the desk."

Pascal smiled with salacious expectation into her silky hair. "Oh, no, my dear. That's not how we're going to manage this."

He felt her sudden tension. "Gervaise?"

"You'll like this. I'd wager another diamond bracelet on it."

He ran his hands down her arms. The oh, so proper satin gloves—well, apart from that vivid red—added extra spice to what he intended. Like stockings on an otherwise naked woman.

He bumped his hips forward, coaxing Amy closer to the desk. Then he stretched her hands across the desk's leather top and flattened them under his. By the time he bent over her, pressing her down, she was trembling.

She guessed his plans now. But then, she was a clever woman.

For a long moment, he paused, his body crushed into the long line of hers and his nose buried in her hair. Her scent, redolent with arousal, was the air he breathed. Her unsteady gasps betrayed uncertainty and excitement.

He kissed the side of her neck. She pushed back in silent invitation.

Fumbling, he released his trousers. Once his cock sprang free to nestle in the tumbling red skirts, he grunted with relief. When she edged back more insistently, he shuddered and bit her neck. She gave a soft cry.

He squeezed her breast, luxuriating in its softness. Then unable to bear the barrier between his hand and her skin, he dipped his fingers under her bodice and found her nipple. Hard and tight with arousal. He tugged on the peak, and she jerked delightfully. With his nail, he teased that sensitive tip until she was shaking.

Only then did he reach down to raise her skirts, bunching them in his hand before tossing them up. When she began to straighten, he placed a hand flat on her lower back. "No. Stay there."

She swung her head to send him a scorching look. "Don't make me wait."

"Never."

What a glorious spectacle she made. Amy Mowbray with her splendid arse in the air. His cock swelled, as his hand traced those luscious curves through her sheer drawers.

A few deft flicks of his fingers, and the cambric crumpled down to drift across her red silk dancing slippers.

"Step out of your drawers," he murmured, bending to place a kiss on one round, satiny cheek, now bare to his sight.

She obeyed immediately and spread her legs. For a long moment, he stared down at her, so pink and glistening and ready. He slid his fingers along her sleek cleft, swiftly finding the place that made her quiver and cry out. When she lifted her hips in silent entreaty, he angled her to take him.

Steadying her with one hand, he positioned his cock with the other. Her choked sound of longing spurred him on. With a powerful glide, he pushed forward.

CHAPTER FOURTEEN

When Gervaise filled her, Amy muffled a cry and pushed back to take him deeper. He bent over her, wrapping his arms around her with such tender care that her heart clenched into an aching fist. Even while her body tightened around him to hold him inside her.

She'd been sure nothing could rival the bliss of what they did in that big bed in his manor. But this exciting variation suggested there were many paths to paradise. What didn't change was the sense that when their bodies joined, somehow their souls joined, too. She'd come to thirst after that feeling of ineffable completion like a drunkard thirsted after brandy.

When Gervaise kissed her neck, a tingly thrill shook her. Then with a languor that sent her up in flames, he withdrew. She felt every inch of that retreat.

Before she could catch her breath, he slammed back into her.

As his ferocious possession shuddered through her, she braced against the desk. This was so different from their previous encounters, but the raw animal vigor stirred her beyond anything she'd ever known.

On his next thrust, her body greeted him with a liquid surge. He growled deep in his throat and bit her neck where before he'd kissed her. Pain vied with pleasure and sent her responses soaring. She closed her eyes and gave herself up to a universe of passion.

The inexorable rhythm built until she turned into his creature, a being of pure sensation. The rapturous end rushed closer and closer, until on another broken cry, coiling suspense snapped into brilliant, incandescent light.

Pascal muttered something incoherent as he pushed her down into the desk with sudden fierceness. Then she felt him jerk against her back, and his hot seed flooded her.

Exhausted, feeling as if she'd walked to Moscow and back, Amy opened dazed eyes. Her cheek pressed against the leather covering the desk, and Gervaise slumped over her. She never wanted to move. Right now, she felt that she and Gervaise inhabited a world where nothing could mar their perfect union.

They were still joined, and soft quivers of pleasure rippled through her. The air smelled of sex and sweat and satisfaction. How could such a flagrantly carnal act make her want to cry at the poignant sweetness of it all?

He groaned as he levered himself up, separating their bodies.

"That was...unforgettable." He sounded shaken, too.

She smiled wearily as she rose. What they'd done had been astonishingly potent, but now she ached from the strenuous mating. Her skirts tumbled down her rubbery legs, restoring a modesty she'd well and truly sacrificed.

Gervaise stepped back, and she turned reluctantly. After that shattering encounter, she felt lost and vulnerable. Only now in the aftermath did she realize what appalling risks they'd taken. This passion for Lord Pascal threatened to carry her into dangerous waters indeed.

When he cupped her cheek, she forced herself to meet his eyes. She wasn't sure what she'd see in his face. Admiration? Fondness? Disgust? She'd just let him debauch her over a desk, for God's sake.

She bit back a gasp. She'd never seen him more beautiful. His blond hair was ruffled, lending him an uncharacteristically boyish air. That long sensual mouth was full and relaxed. And his eyes were clear. He looked young and approachable in a way she'd never seen, even during their radiant hours outside Windsor.

He'd already tucked in his shirt and fastened his trousers, but he was a long way from his usual elegant self. His neck cloth was crushed, and his clothes were crumpled.

"Are you all right?" His thumb brushed her cheek in a caress that she felt to her toes.

"Silly to feel…shy after that." She glanced down to where her drawers lay blatant witness to her wantonness, white against the green and beige carpet. She shifted awkwardly from foot to foot, and the movement reminded her of the slick heat between her legs.

"Not silly at all," he said, with one of those smiles that always made her want to fling herself against him and never let him go.

His kiss immersed her in an ocean of gentleness. She blinked back more foolish tears, even though she still had no real idea why she felt like crying.

Except he sliced through every attempt to defend herself. He left her terrifyingly vulnerable, as though she'd lost a couple of layers of skin. She'd never felt at anyone's mercy, the way she did with Gervaise.

To hide her powerful emotion, she bent to retrieve her drawers. "I'd better take these. Otherwise Lord Frame will get a shock tomorrow morning."

Her voice emerged unnaturally high, and she avoided Gervaise's eyes, although some instinct told her he watched her closely. "Amy?"

"Please turn around." She knew she acted like a ninny, but she felt horridly uncomfortable. The stupid fact was that she'd felt so alive and happy and safe with him pounding into her like a hammer. Now it was over, she was frantic for some privacy to gather her composure. If she appeared in the ballroom, surely everyone must guess exactly what she'd been doing.

She chanced a glance at him. A faint frown marked his face.

"Please," she said with a small, imploring gesture.

His lips compressed with impatience, but he cooperated.

Because her hands shook so badly, she took an age to tie her drawers back on. "You...you can look now," she said in a husky voice.

She'd hoped some poise would return, once she'd got her undergarments off the floor. It didn't.

When Gervaise turned, the eyes that met hers were somber. "I didn't withdraw."

Of course he didn't. Perhaps that was why she was so on edge. Except she'd gloried in that luminous moment when he'd given himself up to her.

"I know," she said in a thready voice.

"I should apologize," he said with a hint of grimness. "But in truth, I don't think I can. It was the most perfect moment of my life."

She searched his face for insincerity, although she was sure he'd always been honest with her. "Really?"

"I know it's a disaster." He sighed and ran his hand through his rumpled hair. "But it doesn't feel like one."

Amy examined her heart. She found confusion, and the constant yearning that by now felt almost like an old friend. But strangely, no regret. Even more unexpected, no fear.

"It doesn't feel like a disaster to me either," she said slowly.

He started to smile. "Well, then."

She frowned. "Well, then, what?"

Gervaise stepped forward and caught one of her gloved hands. "Amy Mowbray, will you make me the happiest man in London and marry me?"

Her heart began to crash about like a drunken sailor. Whether with horror or excitement, she wasn't sure. Probably a turbulent mixture of the two. "Because you're worried about a baby?"

He shook his golden head, and his blue eyes were grave. "I've wanted to marry you from the first. I said so. Don't you remember?"

"I…I didn't think you meant it."

"I told you I was wooing you."

"Into bed."

"Into my bed." He paused. "And my life."

"Oh," she said, wishing she could come up with something more coherent. Tenderness softened his features, and she closed her eyes to delay the inevitable yielding.

"May I kiss you?"

She opened her eyes and pulled away, needing to think. And stupidly missed the contact, the moment it was broken. "You don't usually ask."

"I'm not taking anything for granted."

She liked that. But then, he knew she would. "No, you may not kiss me."

Disappointment dulled his eyes. "Amy, are you saying no to my proposal?"

She hesitated. Was she ready to marry again? If she was, Gervaise would be her choice. But would his interest in her last beyond the illicit excitement of their affair? She couldn't imagine him finding her so fascinating when she went back to being a hardworking farmer. "No."

To her surprise, she watched the jaded mask descend over his features. Even more surprising, she realized she now knew him well enough to recognize that cynicism as a facade. "Then I beg your pardon for troubling you."

A rusty laugh escaped her. "Gervaise, you nitwit. I mean I'm not saying no."

He regarded her uncertainly. "You did."

She shook her head. When they touched, she and Gervaise communicated perfectly. Not so much when they talked, to her regret. "Words are tangling me up."

"Then be clear, for God's sake," he said roughly. "Will you marry me?"

She hesitated, even as she saw her havering tormented him. "I...I'll think about it."

He gave a soft growl of frustration and gestured toward the desk. "After that, you must know how good we are together."

"We desire each other." She swallowed to moisten a dry mouth. "That on its own isn't enough."

"We share more than passion, and you know it. I've never enjoyed a woman's company as I have yours. Don't you like talking to me, too?"

"You know I do." She made a helpless gesture, and decided to take a chance with the prosaic truth. "But London isn't my real life. When the season's over, I'll go back to being eccentric, practical Amy Mowbray, who spends her time tramping her fields and working on improvements to her land and stock."

Gervaise looked offended. "You think I'm too frivolous to hold your attention?"

Her sigh carried the weight of all her years of insecurity. "No, I think I'm too dull to amuse you."

He took her hand again. "What would you say if I told you a life in the country with you at my side sounds like a great adventure?"

Amy frowned, although this time she didn't break free. "I'd say I still need to think." When he loomed closer, she placed her hand on his chest to keep him at bay. "And don't kiss me. You turn my brains to scrambled eggs when you do."

"That's a good thing, when people contemplate marriage," he said, looking happier. Of course he did. He knew now how close she teetered to agreement.

"Not when I need to be sensible." She cringed at the word. It sounded so cramped and mean after this marvelous fortnight of generosity and abundance and passion since she'd gone to his bed.

"You've been sensible your whole life. I'll wager you were born sensible." He placed his hand over hers where it lay above his heart. "Take a chance."

Her laugh was wry. "I was sensible until the day I met you. Now I need a clear head."

He studied her and must have seen that she was adamant. With a sigh, he released her and leaned back against the desk. She tried not to let the dejected slump of his shoulders sway her decision.

"Do you want me to woo you again?"

She found a smile. He sounded like she asked him to sign up for ten years' hard labor in the colonies. "No."

He regarded her under lowered golden brows. "Then for pity's sake, what do you want?"

She wanted him, but that wasn't necessarily a reason to accept him. "I want a couple of days to reflect upon my answer. Surely that's not too much to ask, when we're talking about the rest of our lives."

He straightened, and his expression turned austere. "I'll call tomorrow for your answer," he said in an uncompromising tone.

His sudden ruthlessness startled her. "Gervaise…"

He regarded her impatiently. "You can't pretend my offer comes out of the blue. If you don't know now that we're perfect together, you'll never know. Say yes tomorrow, or send me away forever."

She folded her arms and regarded him with displeasure. "You're very highhanded."

"Get used to it."

The awful truth was that Amy found his arrogance exciting. She didn't want a man who rode roughshod over her. But she respected Gervaise's willingness to stand up to her and demand an answer. Once she'd settled into Warrington Court, she'd become the stronger half of the partnership. Wilfred had followed her every directive. As a result, she'd spent most of her marriage feeling very lonely.

She realized with a shock that when she was with Gervaise, she never felt lonely.

Now she had to deal with this new masterful version of her lover. Heat swirled in her veins, and a familiar sinful longing weighted the base of her belly. What a wanton he made her. She liked this new, daring version of Amy Mowbray.

It was as much to deny that stirring interest as to bring the difficult conversation to a close that she spoke. "We should go. I can hear music. Supper must be over."

He studied her with an unreadable expression before giving her a brief bow as if they returned to the formality of their early meetings. "As you wish."

Actually it wasn't in any way as she wished. Wicked

girl she was, she wanted to stay here with Gervaise and lose herself in mindless pleasure.

More. She wanted him to hustle her away and persuade her with kisses, until she forgot what an important decision marriage was. She had a horrible feeling that if she thought too hard, she'd turn into a coward and scuttle back to obscurity—and safety—in Leicestershire.

Suddenly that seemed a sad outcome to these recent, exciting weeks.

"Am I...am I tidy?" she asked in a reedy voice, as he shrugged on his coat and smoothed his hair. The efficiency of his movements reminded her, as if she needed reminding, that here was a man used to managing amorous intrigues.

His forbidding air softened at her hesitant question, and she sucked in her first full breath since he'd proposed. "Come here," he said gently.

She stood in front of him. He tucked away a couple of stray tendrils of hair and straightened her pretty new dress.

"Will I do?"

"You'll dazzle them all." He leaned forward to give her another of those devastating kisses. He didn't seem angry anymore, but she couldn't forget his ultimatum.

Through the closed door, she heard a quadrille. "I won't dazzle Mr. Harslett. I promised him this dance."

Gervaise's finger traced a burning trail along her jaw. "I wish you could dance with nobody but me."

She raised her eyebrows. "Are you likely to become one of those odiously possessive husbands who snaps like a grumpy dog if his wife flirts with another man?"

His expression turned wry. "You know, I think I am. Does that mean you won't have me?"

"I'm better off knowing," she said lightly. The urge to say yes struggled against the bonds of her prudence. A lifetime with Gervaise? It sounded like heaven. But it seemed despite tonight's rashness, she remained by nature cautious. "Shall we go?"

"Let me check if the corridor is empty." He unlocked the door and edged it open.

She'd started forward when he hauled her back into his arms. They both heard the nearby voices. Amy's heart slammed to a stop, then raced like a runaway horse. She buried her face in Gervaise's chest, as he edged deeper into the shadows behind the open door.

"I can't believe he'd choose her rather than you. You're accounted a diamond of the first water," an affected, very young female voice said in the hallway. Amy didn't recognize the speaker, but she immediately identified the girl who answered.

"He wants her fortune. Mamma says I've had a lucky escape," Lucy Compton-Browne stated with her usual self-satisfaction. Meg had invited the Compton-Browne girl to tea several times. Amy had never much liked her. Or her pushy mother.

"Do you think so? He's so very, very handsome, and

everyone says he's a great catch. Are you sure he has no money?"

Amy felt Gervaise's body turn rigid with tension, and his grip on her tightened.

"Mamma heard it from one of his neighbours, an old school friend who regularly corresponds with her. It's not in general circulation, but it soon will be. People can never keep a story like that secret. A storm last January laid waste to his estates, and apparently he was already up to his ears in debt after a couple of bad harvests. He needs a rich wife, and he needs her quickly."

"Oh, that's a pity when he's such a gorgeous man. If he proposed to me, I don't think I'd care that he's a fortune hunter."

"Have some pride, Arabella. Anyway, Lord Pascal has set his sights on Lady Mowbray—he must have decided a lonely widow without a watchful mamma would be easier prey. I almost feel sorry for her."

"Did you hear something?" the unknown Arabella asked.

Amy bit her lip and cursed her betraying gasp. Through her numbed shock, she was desperate to disentangle herself from Lord Pascal's grasp. Only to find he'd already released her.

"Don't be such a henwit. There's nobody else here. Let's go back to the dancing. Sir Brandon Deerham has requested the next waltz—and he's both handsome and plump in the pocket."

Over the slow death knell playing in her ears, Amy didn't hear anything more. Her stomach knotted into agonizing tangles as she struggled to come to terms with what she'd learned. Blindly she stared at the mahogany door and fumbled for courage, when all she wanted to do was run away and bawl her eyes out.

What an idiot she'd been. A vain, brainless, needy idiot. She knew who she was. She knew who Lord Pascal was. She should immediately have seen that he was out to make a fool of her.

But hindsight provided no comfort and pride couldn't come to her rescue, when her heart was engaged and threatening to break. She made herself look up into that gorgeous, deceiving face. Lord Pascal appeared sick with devastation.

Well, that was what happened when a fortune slipped through your greedy, grasping fingers.

"Is it true?" she asked in a dead voice.

She waited for him to lie. How ironic that not long ago, she'd been convinced that he'd always been honest with her.

He squared his shoulders and met her eyes without flinching. "Yes."

CHAPTER FIFTEEN

*S*ilently, Pascal reached behind him to close the door. The click of the latch sounded loud in the reverberant silence.

He went across to fill two glasses of brandy. He passed one to Amy who had followed him, then drained his, before returning it to the sideboard. He performed every action with exaggerated care, as if somehow close attention now could make up for his wrongs against her.

Beneath his surface calm writhed lacerating regret. Regret that he'd hurt her. Regret that he was sure to lose her. Regret that she'd never believe him now, when he told her how he treasured her. The pain was so sharp, it was like rats gnawing at his guts.

He deserved it, he supposed. But Amy didn't. That was the hell of it.

The liquor burned a path down his throat, but

didn't banish his stark memory of her frozen horror when she learned the truth. He braced for her to speak, to storm at him, to accuse him of being a fortune hunter. But she stood silent in the middle of the room.

Her expression was hard to read. He'd seen her immediate, stabbing hurt. Now she'd drawn her formidable defenses tight around her. She was proud and pale, back straight as a ruler and head held high. And as beautiful as he'd ever seen her.

After she sent him away, as she surely must, this was how he'd remember her.

Instead of drinking the brandy, she set her glass on the desk with an unsteady hand. Her accusing gaze leveled on him. "Tell me, Gervaise."

Pascal found no encouragement in her use of his Christian name. He made a despairing gesture as guilt lashed at him. "It will all sound so hellishly bad."

Her lips twisted. "Did you ever intend to admit you were after my money?"

He bit back a furious protest. Because of course, that was how it had all started, wasn't it? "Yes."

"When?" For the first time, outrage edged her voice. But he wasn't fooled about what she felt. Any anger stemmed from her anguish at his betrayal. "After we were married, and the settlements were signed, and you had your hands on my fortune?"

He shook his head in bleak denial, although in truth he'd never decided when to reveal his financial embarrassment. He should have told her from the first. She'd have marched away with that damned purposeful strut he loved, but at least she wouldn't condemn him as a liar.

Pascal swallowed to push down the remorse crammed in his throat. "Please, sit down."

She didn't move. "Do you think you can charm me into ignoring this?"

Again he shook his head. "No. But I'd at least like you to understand, before you consign me to the devil."

He didn't exaggerate. Life without her was going to be the closest thing to hell he'd experience this side of the grave. But now she was convinced he'd lied from the first, she'd never believe his feelings were sincere.

The curse of all liars.

"If you insist." Without shifting her gaze from him, she sank down onto the couch.

Resisting the urge to have another brandy, he crossed to sit beside her. No amount of brandy was going to soothe this pain. She shot him a warning glance, but he didn't need any reminder that his touch was no longer welcome.

A heavy silence crashed down. Pascal stared sightlessly at the carpet and fisted his hands on his thighs. There was a clock on the mantel, and its heavy ticking threatened to send him mad. The lilting music from the ballroom seemed to come from another world.

"Please put me out of my misery," Amy said, in a low voice that would have broken his heart, if it wasn't broken already. "Was it all a pretense? Every bit of it? Right from the very beginning?"

There was little he could say to defend himself, but he couldn't bear to let her go, believing that his seduction had been cold and calculated. "No. No, it wasn't like that. On my honor, I swear it wasn't."

He looked up and met her eyes. The bright hazel turned a dull, muddy brown. He loathed that he'd made this vivid creature so wretched.

"You speak of honor?"

His mouth curved down in corrosive self-hatred. "You have every right to despise me."

"Gervaise, I can take it. Whatever the full story is." She still spoke in that calm voice. He'd feel better if she shouted and wept. "Just tell me. And don't lie."

Sucking in a shuddering breath, he went back to studying the carpet. He couldn't endure seeing her regard turn to contempt. In recent days he'd imagined —hoped—he looked into her eyes and saw love.

"The Compton-Browne chit is right." His flat voice masked the acrid desolation eating at him. "I badly need money to repair the damage to my estate. We had a hurricane through last winter. I believe the place will recover and become profitable again. It's good land, and the tenants are hardworking."

"But right now it's a mess," she said, and he recalled that she'd been a farmer most of her life. At least he didn't need to describe the toll on life and property the storm had taken. "I understand."

He tensed his fists against rising despair. He could sink into the mire of his sins once she'd left him. Now he needed to concentrate on giving her an explanation, however badly he emerged from the tale. "So I came to Town, seeking a rich wife. I'm thirty. It was time to set up my nursery anyway."

"Very pragmatic."

He ignored her acerbic response. "I'm not saying I wanted to marry. You know I've been a libertine."

"I know," she said, in a hollow tone that crushed his heart to the size of a walnut. He ached to offer her comfort, but what comfort could she accept from the man who'd hurt her so unforgivably?

He forced himself to continue, although every word of his confession made his skin crawl. "I started my hunt with the current crop of debutantes, but, Lord above, they're a henwitted bunch. Silliest gaggle of chits to arrive on the marriage mart in ten years. The night I met you, I was trying to choose between offering for Cissie Veivers, or going home and cutting my throat. When I saw you across that ballroom, you were the answer to a prayer."

"Plump in the pocket, and too naïve to question your sudden unlikely interest?"

His self-loathing sharpened to agony. She'd be better off if he had cut his throat after the Raynor ball. Over the last weeks, he'd loved watching as her confidence blossomed. Now he'd destroyed it. What a bastard he was.

And still he had to finish this deuced excruciating account. "I remember saying to myself, after yet another soporific conversation with Miss Veivers, that I'd sell my soul for a sensible woman past first youth who had the money to restore my lands."

"And your prayers were answered," she said bitterly. "Although I wouldn't describe my recent behavior as sensible."

He sighed. "It's my damned selfishness. All my life, what I've wanted has dropped into my lap. Often I haven't even taken the trouble to ask for it. When I saw you, and you were so exactly the right wife for me, I assumed ever-reliable fate operated once more to my advantage."

"Lucky you."

He winced at her sarcasm. "No. All that good fortune made me shallow."

Her restive hands pleated her skirts. Part of him wished she'd just hit him. She'd feel better if she unleashed the turmoil roiling beneath her unnatural composure.

"Not...shallow," she said slowly. "Thoughtless perhaps."

"That's not much better." The need to take her hand in his was torture. Hell, everything right now was torture.

She was still pale as rice paper. He beat back the memory of how she'd looked after he'd taken her. Rosy with satisfaction. Brilliant with happiness. He couldn't endure the contrast with this sad woman beside him now.

"So your plan came to fruition. You saw me, and lured me in, and had your way with me." Vinegar crept into her voice. "I should have guessed a man like you wouldn't pursue a woman like me without some underlying motive."

"Amy, no," he protested, and this time he couldn't resist seizing her fretful hand. "One of the reasons I delayed telling you is that I knew this is what you'd think. But you're wrong."

She wrenched free, and he had to let her go. "No, I'm not."

"You are."

The hard-eyed gaze she settled on him penetrated his deceptively appealing exterior to the shameful sins beneath. "Prove it."

He should be grateful she gave him a chance to explain, although he was all too conscious that words were inadequate to heal the injury he'd done her. But words were all that were left to him. He'd have to do his best. He owed her any recompense he could make. Even if none of it was enough.

Drawing a shaky breath, Pascal faced up to the disaster he'd made of the most important relationship in his useless life.

He'd always skated by on charm and looks. It had been enough for everyone else he knew. It wasn't good enough for Amy.

"I liked you from the first. You must believe that. You were clever and interesting, and you didn't make cow eyes at me or giggle."

"I should hope not."

"And you were so lovely—and unaware of your attractions, which made you even more appealing."

"Because I was ripe for duping?"

Hell, she was a million miles from forgiving him. He reached a point where her forgiveness was all he hoped for—with no great optimism that he'd receive it. His machinations had put anything more forever out of reach. Knowing it was his own fault that he reached this impasse made him want to smash his fist through a window.

"No. Because I live in a world of appearances and lies, and you're so rare and true. How in Hades could I resist you?"

He waited for Amy to challenge that statement, but she remained silent. He forced himself to go on. "In my conceit, I thought you were drawn to me, the way I was drawn to you."

"Well, I kissed you when we weren't much beyond strangers." The shame in her voice made him flinch. "What else would you think?"

"What I thought was that I was in trouble. Even that first night, my self-serving plan was under threat. You made me feel things I'd never felt before. I should have taken to my heels then and there. But already I was enchanted."

"With my fortune."

"No, with you. With your quirky humor, and lovely face, and quick passion." He paused. "And your lonely, steadfast heart."

It was her turn to flinch. For the first time, she looked away from him. "I refuse to discuss my lonely, steadfast heart."

"But don't you see?" He jerked to his feet. He couldn't sit beside her any longer without hauling her into his arms. "I've been lonely, too."

"You?" She stared up at him with blatant disbelief.

Good God, she stripped his black soul bare. "London's handsomest man doesn't have friends. He has admirers."

"Oh, Gervaise…"

Pascal recoiled from the pity in her eyes and ran a shaking hand through his hair. "But you didn't tumble into my arms like every other woman I've ever wanted." He drew himself up to his full height, as if he faced an executioner. In terms of his future happiness, he supposed he did. "You made me work for my victory. You made me prove myself. I learned to respect you."

"Then I tumbled anyway. So much for respect."

"Don't be a fool, Amy," he said shortly. "I've never been so happy in my life as I've been this last fortnight with you."

She still studied him as if she weighed every word. She weighed his soul, too. He suffered the wretched certainty that his soul came up lacking. "You almost sound as if you mean that."

He made a frustrated gesture. "Of course I bloody mean it."

"So what are you saying?" She stood up too, more circumspectly than he had. "That you started this pursuit to gain my fortune, but you've since developed a genuine affection for me?"

His grunt of laughter held no amusement. "Oh, my darling, it's much, much worse than that."

He watched her prepare for another blow. "You've told me most of it. You may as well tell me everything."

Sheer terror cramped his gut. His skin itched. Right now, he'd give every penny of his depleted fortune to avoid the last, most painful confession. This situation called for a man of character—and he'd never been that.

But he had to go on, whatever happened next.

His voice emerged as a growl. "I don't just like and respect and desire you. I don't just want to be your friend and your lover."

"No, you want to be my banker," she retorted.

He ignored her astringent interjection, too busy summoning every ragtag shred of courage to make the last, humiliating revelation. "I've fallen head over heels with you, Amy. My life without you will be a barren waste." Then he spoke words he'd never said before, words he never thought he'd say to anyone. "I love you."

Aghast, Amy retreated until her legs bumped the couch. Her knees felt weak and shaky. To stay upright, she fumbled for the back of the couch. She felt so horridly lost and confused. Tonight she'd been through a storm to rival the hurricane that destroyed Gervaise's fortune. She'd jolted from ecstasy to betrayal and anguish.

And now this, the ultimate shock.

In all their time together, she'd never imagined him saying such a thing to her.

Did he mean it? Could she trust him? Her gaze clung to that austere, perfect face. He looked desperately unhappy, and a muscle flickered in his cheek. He gave every appearance of a man on the emotional edge.

Was that because he was about to lose Amy Mowbray? Or Amy Mowbray's substantial fortune?

"That's easy to say," she said sharply.

His smile was sour. "No, it isn't. And the devil of it is I mean it to my soul, yet you'll never believe it's true."

Still she studied him, her vision at last free of the deceiving veils of glamour and girlhood fantasy. For the first time, his extraordinary looks weren't what captured her attention. Instead she finally saw the fallible man beneath his superb shell.

So where did that leave her? Did fallible mean irredeemable? Or was there a whisper of goodness skulking under his spectacular hide?

For the last few weeks, desire had steered her usually reliable brain. But now, she started to think. She needed to winnow the truth from the lies. If there was any truth there at all. "Why didn't you tell me about your estate?"

He sighed. "Because you doubted yourself so completely, you'd immediately assume the only reason I pursued you was for your money. And that's exactly what's happened, damn it."

To her surprise, as she witnessed what looked like genuine distress, part of her suspected he wasn't entirely false. At least not all the time. "After tonight, I think a tiny corner of you holds some honest regard for me."

He cast her an astonished glance. "Really?"

She shrugged and dared to take a step toward him. "Apparently my affair with the much sought-after Lord Pascal has done wonders for my confidence."

He frowned, as if seeking some hidden attack in her words. "But how the devil can I ever convince you I don't want your money?"

"I thought you did want it."

His smile was grim. "I do. But not as much as I want you."

She almost—*almost*—believed him. "We could put it in trust for our children."

He looked brighter. "We could. That's an excellent idea. We might have to live quietly in the country for a couple of years. Watch our pennies. Do the urgent tasks first, and leave the rest until we can afford it. I'm sure if we make some economies on the estate, we'll manage."

"We could work something out, that's certain."

"Amy?" Gervaise regarded her as if he still didn't trust what she said. He'd been so sunk in self-hatred and misery, she couldn't blame him.

"And you're marrying a woman famous for her scientific approach to farming. Once I get my hands on it, your estate will be a showplace in no time."

The flare of hope in his eyes set her heart racing and skipping and jumping. She sent up a tiny, urgent prayer. *Dear Lord, don't let this be another trick.*

He'd lied to her. That was irrefutable. But did that mean everything was lies?

Her brain had come to her rescue, thank heaven. And reminded her of what she and Gervaise had shared.

While his motives had undeniably been murky, Amy couldn't dismiss all his actions as callous self-interest. She remembered how desperate he'd been for her, and how careful when he'd taken her. And how desolate he'd looked when he thought he'd lost her.

She remembered, too, how amiably he'd devoted a day to tramping around Sir Godfrey Yelland's muddy farm, just because she wanted to look at cattle. She remembered his kindness and his humor. And how he'd entrusted her with the sad story of his childhood, when it was clear the humiliating details left his pride in tatters.

She remembered the times—until tonight when he'd been mad for her—he'd protected her from conceiving. When a pregnancy was the quickest, surest way to gain her consent to a wedding.

She remembered how mad he'd been for her tonight.

Gervaise's stare was unwavering, as if he was a condemned man, and only she could save him from a hanging.

"The tragic truth is that's why I want to marry you —all that free advice." He struggled to achieve his usual sardonic note. It was a little too threadbare to be convincing. But the small, dry joke hinted that he crawled out of his despair.

She prayed that he really was in despair, and this wasn't more deception. But some bone-deep instinct insisted that he wouldn't betray her again. That he might have started out after her fortune, but against all the odds, now he really did love her.

He loved her.

Was she prepared to take the greatest risk of her life? By now, she should be used to this giddy mixture of dread and excitement. She'd felt this way since the day she met him again.

"You know, if you'd offered me the chance to bring an ailing estate back to prosperity, I'd have married you when you first proposed."

"I'll remember that for the next time I find a woman I want to make my wife."

Although it was cursed difficult to look stern when a chorus of larks trilled in her soul, she summoned a frown. "You'd better not, or there will be trouble."

"Why?"

Amy decided that in the end, all she could do was trust her heart. Her brain would take her so far, but it wouldn't give her the courage to seize the future she wanted. A future with Gervaise at her side.

She stood straight and tall and met his eyes. "Because the only woman you're going to marry is right in front of you."

Incredulity flooded his face, then swift, over-whelming relief that filled her with thankfulness. They might just pull through this crisis and find their way back to one another.

In breathless suspense, she waited for him to sweep her up and tell her how happy he was, but he folded his arms and studied her down his aristocratic nose. "Why?"

Her lips twitched, when not long ago, she thought she'd never smile again. "Because after you've played reckless games with my heart and honor, you deserve to suffer."

"Amy," he said implacably. The glittering brightness of his eyes spoiled the effect a tad. She read hope in his expression, but he wasn't yet ready to trust that he'd won.

"Because I want to devote my fortune to restoring yours."

He shook his head in disapproval. "I told you—I don't want your blasted money. If I take it, you'll never trust me. I'd rather have you."

"You'll have me."

Still he didn't relent. "Then let me put it another way. I'd rather have your love. Do you love me?"

She caught a glimpse of the aching vulnerability beneath his masterful pose, and all impulse to tease faded. Because of course she loved him. She'd loved him since she was a silly fourteen-year-old at Woodley Park.

There had been enough secrets between them. Secrets had nearly torn them apart.

Amy squared her shoulders and sucked in a deep breath. "Yes."

Joy flared in his eyes, but still he didn't kiss her. What the devil was wrong with him? "I didn't hear you."

She stepped closer. "Yes," she said more loudly.

"Yes, what?"

"Oh, you're a scoundrel."

He tilted one eyebrow.

She sighed and gave in. "Very well. I love you, too."

He didn't smile, but the taut line of his shoulders relaxed, and the deep lines running between his nose and mouth eased. "God, I hope so."

She spread her hands in a helpless gesture. "How

could I do anything but love you? Nobody else makes me feel the way you do."

The unabashed longing in his face made her tremble. "And you'll marry me?"

"I will." She raised her chin and glared. "Although I'll change my mind, if you don't kiss me this very minute."

At last, a spark of genuine amusement lit his expression. "Well, we can't have that."

Before she could respond, he dragged her into his arms and kissed her with a passion beyond anything she'd ever known. Perhaps because they'd come so close to losing one another. He was trembling, too, she was moved to discover. And realizing that, the last of her doubts melted into the air. She clung to him and gave herself up to the miraculous truth that they were in love, and they were going to share a life together.

When much later she returned to the real world, they were sitting on the sofa, and she was twined around him, breathless and happy. Gervaise brought her head down to rest on his shoulder and pressed a kiss to her rumpled hair. His tenderness carved a rift in her heart. From the first, that tenderness had hinted that he wasn't quite the selfish rogue he liked to believe.

"Did I tell you I love you?" he murmured.

She cuddled closer to his radiant heat. "You can definitely tell me again."

"I love you." The sweetness in his kiss turned her bones to syrup.

"And I love you." She raised her head and stared into his face. She saw a strength that would sustain her for the rest of her life. "Forever."

With a brilliant smile, he untangled himself. He stood and stretched out his hand. "Then, my lovely Amy, come away with me now, and let's enjoy a purely private celebration. Tomorrow, we'll tell the world, but tonight is for us alone."

"Won't that cause talk?" she asked, even as anticipation ripped through her.

He shrugged. "Let them gossip. I need to have you in my arms."

How marvelously scandalous. She loved it. But not as much as she loved him.

Amy's fingers curled around Gervaise's, and she let him draw her to her feet. "That's an invitation I can't resist, my darling Lord Pascal."

ABOUT THE AUTHOR

ANNA CAMPBELL has written 10 multi award-winning historical romances for Grand Central Publishing and Avon HarperCollins, and her work is published in 22 languages. She has also written 21 bestselling independently published romances, including her series, The Dashing Widows and The Lairds Most Likely. Anna has won numerous awards for her Regency-set stories including Romantic Times Reviewers Choice, the Booksellers Best, the Golden Quill (three times), the Heart of Excellence (twice), the Write Touch, the Aspen Gold (twice) and the Australian Romance Readers Association's favorite historical romance (five times). Her books have three times been nominated for Romance Writers of America's prestigious RITA Award, and three times for Australia's Romantic Book of the Year. When she's not traveling the world seeking inspiration for her stories, Anna lives on the beautiful east coast of Australia.

Anna loves to hear from her readers. You can find her at:

Website: www.annacampbell.com

ALSO BY ANNA CAMPBELL

Claiming the Courtesan

Untouched

Tempt the Devil

Captive of Sin

My Reckless Surrender

Midnight's Wild Passion

The Sons of Sin series:

Seven Nights in a Rogue's Bed

Days of Rakes and Roses

A Rake's Midnight Kiss

What a Duke Dares

A Scoundrel by Moonlight

Three Proposals and a Scandal

The Dashing Widows:

The Seduction of Lord Stone

Tempting Mr. Townsend

Winning Lord West

Pursuing Lord Pascal

Charming Sir Charles

Catching Captain Nash

Lord Garson's Bride

The Lairds Most Likely:

The Laird's Willful Lass

The Laird's Christmas Kiss

The Highlander's Lost Lady

Christmas Stories:

The Winter Wife

Her Christmas Earl

A Pirate for Christmas

Mistletoe and the Major

A Match Made in Mistletoe

The Christmas Stranger

Other Books:

These Haunted Hearts

Stranded with the Scottish Earl

THE SEDUCTION OF LORD STONE

(The Dashing Widows Book 1)

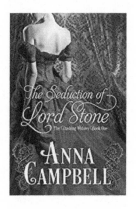

For this reckless widow, love is the most dangerous game of all.

Caroline, Lady Beaumont, arrives in London seeking excitement after ten dreary years of marriage and an even drearier year of mourning. That means conquering society, dancing like there's no tomorrow, and taking a lover to provide passion without promises. Promises, in this dashing widow's dictionary, equal prison. So what is an adventurous lady to do when she loses her heart to a notorious rake who, for the first time in his life, wants forever?

Devilish Silas Nash, Viscount Stone is in love at last with a beautiful, headstrong widow bent on playing the field. Worse, she's enlisted his help to set her up with his disreputable best friend. No red-blooded man takes such a challenge lying down, and Silas schemes to seduce his darling into his arms, warm, willing and besotted. But will his passionate plots come undone against a woman determined to act the mistress, but never the wife?

TEMPTING MR TOWNSEND

(The Dashing Widows Book 2)

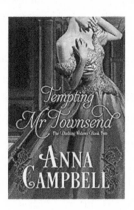

Beauty...

Fenella, Lady Deerham has rejoined society after five years
of mourning her beloved husband's death at Waterloo. Now
she's fêted as a diamond of the first water and London's
perfect lady. But beneath her exquisite exterior, this delicate
blond beauty conceals depths of courage and passion nobody
has ever suspected. When her son and his school friend go
missing, she vows to find them whatever it takes. Including
setting off alone in the middle of the night with high-handed
bear of a man, Anthony Townsend.

Will this tumultuous journey end in more tragedy? Or will
the impetuous quest astonish this Dashing Widow with a
breathtaking new love, and life with the last man she ever
imagined?

And the Beast?

When Anthony Townsend bursts into Lady Deerham's fashionable Mayfair mansion demanding the return of his orphaned nephew, the lovely widow's beauty and spirit turn his world upside down. But surely such a refined and aristocratic creature will scorn a rough, self-made man's courtship, even if that man is now one of the richest magnates in England. Especially after he's made such a woeful first impression by barging into her house and accusing her of conniving with the runaways. But when Fenella insists on sharing the desperate search for the boys, fate offers Anthony a chance to play the hero and change her mind about him.

Will reluctant proximity convince Fenella that perhaps Mr. Townsend isn't so beastly after all? Or now that their charges are safe, will Anthony and Fenella remain forever opposites fighting their attraction?

WINNING LORD WEST

(The Dashing Widows Book 3)

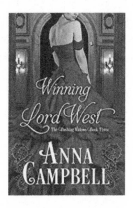

All rakes are the same! Except when they're not...

Spirited Helena, Countess of Crewe, knows all about
profligate rakes; she was married to one for nine years and
still bears the scars. Now this Dashing Widow plans a life of
glorious freedom where she does just what she wishes – and
nobody will ever hurt her again.

So what is she to do when that handsome scoundrel Lord
West sets out to make her his wife? Say no, of course. Which
is fine, until West focuses all his sensual skills on changing
her mind. And West's sensual skills are renowned far and
wide as utterly irresistible...

Passionate persuasion!

Vernon Grange, Lord West, has long been estranged from his
headstrong first love, Helena Nash, but he's always regretted
that he didn't step in to prevent her disastrous marriage.

Now Helena is free, and this time, come hell or high water, West won't let her escape him again.

His weapon of choice is seduction, and in this particular game, he's an acknowledged master. Now that he and Helena are under one roof at the year's most glamorous house party, he intends to counter her every argument with breathtaking pleasure. Could it be that Lady Crewe's dashing days are numbered?

CHARMING SIR CHARLES

(The Dashing Widows Book 5)

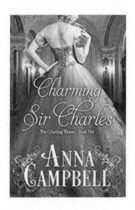

Matchmaking mayhem in Mayfair!

Sally Cowan, Countess of Norwood, spent ten miserable years married to an overbearing oaf. Now she's free, she plans to have some fun. But before she kicks her heels up, this Dashing Widow sets out to launch her pretty, headstrong niece Meg into society and find her a good husband.

When rich and charming Sir Charles Kinglake gives every sign that he can't get enough of Meg's company, Sally is delighted to play chaperone at all their meetings. Charles is everything that's desirable in a gentleman suitor. How disastrous, when over the course of the season's most elegant house party, Sally realizes that desire is precisely the name of the game. She's found her niece's perfect match—but she wants him for herself!

There are none so blind as those who will not see...

From the moment Sir Charles Kinglake meets sparkling Lady Norwood, he's smitten. He courts her as a gentleman should—dancing with her at every glittering ball, taking her to the theatre, escorting her around London. Because she's acting as chaperone to her niece, that means most times, Meg accompanies them. The lack of privacy chafes a man consumed by desire, but Charles's intentions are honorable, and he's willing to work within the rules to win the wife he wants.

However when he discovers that his careful pursuit has convinced Sally he's interested in Meg rather than her, he flings the rules out the window. When love is at stake, who cares about a little scandal? It's time for charming Sir Charles to abandon the subtle approach and play the passionate lover, not the society suitor!

Now with everything at sixes and sevens, Sir Charles risks everything to show lovely Lady Norwood they make the perfect pair!

CATCHING CAPTAIN NASH

(The Dashing Widows Book 6)

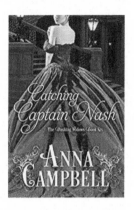

Home is the sailor, home from the sea...

Five years after he's lost off the coast of South America,
presumed dead, Captain Robert Nash escapes cruel captivity,
and returns to London and the bride he loves, but barely
knows. When he stumbles back into the family home, he's
appalled to find himself gate-crashing the party celebrating
his wife's engagement to another man.

This gallant naval officer is ready to take on any challenge;
but five years is a long time, and beautiful, passionate
Morwenna has clearly found a life without him. Can he win
back the wife who gave him a reason to survive his ordeal?
Or will the woman who haunts his every thought remain
eternally out of reach?

Love lost and found? Or love lost forever?

Since hearing of her beloved husband's death, Morwenna

Nash has been mired in grief. After five bleak years without him, she must summon every ounce of courage and determination to become a Dashing Widow and rejoin the social whirl. She owes it to her young daughter to break free of old sorrow and find a new purpose in life, even if that means accepting a loveless marriage.

It's a miracle when Robert returns from the grave, and despite the awkward circumstances of his arrival, she's overjoyed that her husband has come back to her at last. But after years of suffering, he's not the handsome, laughing charmer she remembers. Instead he's a grim shadow of his former dashing self. He can't hide how much he still wants her—but does passion equal love?

Can Morwenna and Robert bridge the chasm of absence, suffering and mistrust, and find their way back to each other?

LORD GARSON'S BRIDE

(The Dashing Widows Book 7)

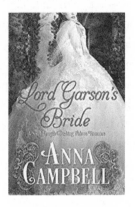

Lord Garson's dilemma.

Hugh Rutherford, Lord Garson, loved and lost when his
fiancée returned to the husband she'd believed drowned. In
the three years since, Garson has come to loathe his
notoriety as London's most famous rejected suitor. It's high
time to find a bride, a level-headed, well-bred lady who will
accept a loveless marriage and cause no trouble. Luckily he
has just the candidate in mind.

A marriage of convenience...

When Lady Jane Norris receives an unexpected proposal
from her childhood friend Lord Garson, marriage to the
handsome baron rescues her from a grim future. At twenty-
eight, Jane is on the shelf and under no illusions about her
attractions. With her father's death, she's lost her home and
faces life as an impecunious spinster. While she's aware

Garson will never love again, they have friendship and goodwill to build upon. What can possibly go wrong?

...becomes very inconvenient indeed.

From the first, things don't go to plan, not least because Garson soon finds himself in thrall to his surprisingly intriguing bride. A union grounded in duty veers toward obsession. And when the Dashing Widows take Jane in hand and transform her into the toast of London, Garson isn't the only man to notice his wife's beauty and charm. He's known Jane all her life, but suddenly she's a dazzling stranger. This isn't the uncomplicated, pragmatic match he signed up for. When Jane defies the final taboo and asks for his love, her impossible demand threatens to blast this convenient marriage to oblivion.

Once the dust settles, will Lord Garson still be the man who can only love once?

Made in the USA
Coppell, TX
20 August 2020

33769086R00135